Malefison

A teenage boy soon realizes he has magical powers way beyond his imagination. He must set out to find out how and why he has gained these powers on his 13th Birthday. He unravels a mysterious past that is linked to Disneyland.

A must read!!!

Believe in your dreams and what you can do.
For one day, they might just come true.

-Braxton

Malefison

Braxton husk

Chapter 1

Rose was absently aware of the smell of brewing coffee, as she began to worry.

"I don't think it's such a good idea to go on a trip right before we have the baby."

She was a beautiful young woman with lovely brown hair that was always styled in curls, with the occasional bow. "Nonsense, this will help you relax. After all, the baby isn't due for another two weeks," said William.

William was a handsome young man with a strong jaw, and slicked back black hair like the style from the movie, *Grease*, or the 1950s.

"Yeah, I guess." Rose said with a worried look on her face. "But what if the baby comes early?"

"It's nothing to be afraid of. If he or she comes early, then I'm sure there will be an emergency room somewhere close," William said, trying to keep Rose calm.

"But, by the way, why didn't we go get an ultrasound?"

"Oh, I just wanted to be surprised when the baby was born…" Rose froze and looked at William.

"It's… It's coming!"

"Oh no, oh no, no, no!" William cried, with sweat dripping from his slicked back black hair.

"Hold tight! I'm gonna go get the phone to call an ambulance!"

William dropped the clothes he was about to pack and ran to the kitchen to grab his phone. Rushing back to the living room, already dialing 911, he stopped. Rose was just sitting there, calmly packing her clothes again.

"Wait, what? What… what happened? Are you okay?"

"Yes, Will, I'm fine. You would have known that if you weren't screaming like a banshee to grab your phone. I yelled out I was okay."

"Oh!" William said with an embarrassed look on his face.

Sweat was still dripping down his chin, until it was about to hit the carpet.

"Well, then…" said William, wiping the sweat off his face.

"Just get back to packing. Isn't the plane leaving this morning?" Rose asked, with a confused look on her face.

William turned to look at the clock on the wall. It read 6:30 a.m.

"Oh, yeah, I forgot it was so early, because of all the rushing that you might be having the baby, right here on the spot…

no big deal." William said, chuckling a little as he said it.

"But we're not flying. Where we're going is only a few miles away." He threw his phone onto the couch, hoping it wouldn't hit the side and bounce off onto the floor.

"Geez, Will, you're gonna break your phone one of these days if you're not careful," Rose said sternly.

"Okay, I'm sorry. I won't do it again." He frowned at Rose like she was his mother.

"Where are we going again, exactly?" Asked Rose curiously, still packing her clothes into a suitcase that was about to burst.

"Disneyland!" William said, with a massive smile on his face.

"Okay, hon, but isn't that place a little too… I don't know, childish for us?"

"No! It's the happiest place on earth!"

A few hours passed and it was finally time for William and Rose to get into the car. William saw something shining on Rose's neck. It was a necklace with a four-leaf clover symbol on it.

"What's that?" William asked, as he reached over the center console and put half of the necklace into his palm to examine it. "How come I haven't seen this before?"

"Oh, I usually keep it inside my shirt, just in case," Rose said, looking at the necklace smiling. "It was my mother's."

"Oh, the Evil Queen?" William said, giggling.

"Shut up," Rose said, giggling as well.

"But seriously, I loved your mom. She was always so nice," William said.

"Yeah, looking at this necklace just brings back so many memories," Rose said, as she started tearing up.

William thought to himself, *oh yeah, I forgot about the hormones.*

"It's okay. She's in a better place now, but now we're going to a better place, too! Disneyland!"

William pressed the gas pedal as they headed down the driveway.

"Wow, you seriously are really excited about this, aren't you?" Rose asked smiling, wiping the tears off her face.

"Yup!" William said, driving down the road, taking a corner turn down the street, which led to the exit of the suburban neighborhood where every house had the same features.

"We're here!" William shouted, entering the parking lot of the resort and parks.

As they exited from the driver and passenger sides of the car, Rose struggled to get out. William ran over to help her out. After checking in and getting their room key, Rose sat heavily on the bed as William put the luggage in the room.

"Okay, let's head to the park," said William, as they walked to the entrance of the Disneyland resort.

Rose couldn't help but get excited, but she kept it to herself. Rose and William looked at the train station's clock. It read 12 p.m. Right on time, the Disneyland train blew its horn. Rose jumped and William laughed.

"Geez, that was loud," Rose said.

"Yeah, just like your shirt!" William let out a laugh.

Rose lightly punched William in the shoulder.

"I'm just kidding. You look beautiful." William kissed Rose on the forehead.

"Oh, yeah, here!" William said, pulling tickets to the park out and handing one to Rose.

"Aww, it's Minnie. She was always my favorite," Rose said, smiling and giving William a warm hug from the side.

"Sorry, I would have given you a front hug, but you know, I'm kinda pregnant." Rose giggled at the same time as William.

"Yeah, I got Mickey Mouse. He was always my favorite." William said, smiling as he stood on his toes to look over the crowd and see how much longer the line was going to be.

Rose and William finally made it to the front of the line a few minutes later.

"Finally, I'm starving. Can we get something to eat before we hit any of the rides?"

"Sure, I know of a great place," William said.

Rose handed her Minnie Mouse card to the cast member scanning the barcodes, and William followed soon after. As they walked under the railroad through a tunnel with posters of popular Disney rides, Rose and William heard a faint, "When you wish upon a star..."

As they entered the park, they saw the Emporium and walked around it to see Sleeping Beauty's Castle standing high and proud over Disneyland.

"Wow! It looks more beautiful than I remember!" Rose said with a jolt of excitement.

"I knew you would love it!" Said William, while he was having his own little moment taking in the scenery.

Rose ran into the middle of Main Street, shouting at William to take her photo in front of the castle. Wearing an old Disneyland short-sleeved shirt from when she was a kid, Rose stood with her belly poking out. It was a good thing she bought a large back then.

Wearing blue jeans and sandals, her beautiful brunette hair tied up into a bun, she looked radiant. William pulled his Polaroid camera that was hanging around his neck for safekeeping from his chest.

"Got it!" William shouted.

"Okay, Tinker Bell, let's go eat at that place I was talking about," said William. As they walked down Main Street, Rose was amazed with how beautiful all the scenery was. They finally arrived at the end of Main Street, where to the left they saw the Corner Café.

"This is it!" William exclaimed.

"Yes, I can seriously go for a hot dog right now!" Rose replied.

There was no line when they walked in, so William began to order.

Rose cut him off, saying, "Hi! I would like two extra-large hot dogs, two cold pickles, a large order of French fries, and a large Pepsi, please."

"Okay, then… Just give me a small order of French fries."

As they sat under an umbrella in front of the restaurant, William grabbed a map of the park to plan out their day.

William said, "How about we ride Peter Pan's Flight first, It's A Small World second, Storybook Land Canal Boats third, and…"

William looked up and noticed that Rose had already eaten one and a half hot dogs, the whole order of fries, and one pickle. Plus, she had drunk two-thirds of the Pepsi.

As she was about to take another bite of the hot dog, she looked up at William and said, "What are you looking at?" She laughed, and William quickly looked down at the map.

"You know I'm just playing, Will," She said, still giggling.

"Yeah, well you looked like you were about to chuck what was left of your hot dog at my face."

They both laughed hysterically, while people watched them as if they were crazy.

While Rose was putting what was left of their food into a trashcan near their table, William got up to join her. Rose and William soon started walking down Main Street once again. The road curved left and then right into a circle that surrounded Walt Disney's Partners statue, where Walt and Mickey were holding hands while gazing onto Main Street. William decided to walk up to the statue and take a picture of it. Once he was done, Rose and William walked around the statue where they saw the drawbridge leading to the doorway for Sleeping Beauty's Castle. Rose and William both looked through the entrance of the castle to see the King Arthur Carrousel. They looked at each other as William grabbed Rose's hand, and they walked over the drawbridge, through the castle corridor, and into Fantasyland.

As both Rose and William walked through the part of Fantasyland directly behind the castle, they saw the rides — Peter Pan's Flight, Snow White's Scary Adventure, and the King Arthur Carrousel — right in the heart of the Disneyland Park.

Chapter 2

"What ride should we go on first?" Rose asked, looking at all the rides Fantasyland had to offer on the Disneyland map.

William looked at the map and said, "Let's go on It's A Small World."

"Not yet. That's all the way in the back towards Toontown. Let's pick something close, then we can make our way down there as we go." Rose pointed to the ride on the map.

"Okay, then, what ride should we ride first?" Asked William, while people walked around them.

"Peter Pan's Flight!" Rose shouted.

"I loved that movie so much when I was a kid!" Rose said excitedly.

"Now you're in the spirit!" William exclaimed, getting very excited as well.

As they walked over to the ride, they noticed there would be an hour's wait for it.

"Dang, a whole hour, Will. Should we pick a different ride?"

"Not to worry. Look at the card I gave you at the front gate."

"Okay…?" Rose said, with a confused look on her face.

"Look closer," said William.

Rose looked more closely at the card and saw that it read "Fast-Pass." Rose let out a big cheer as she hugged William.

"I thought we should get Fast-Passes since we were gonna be here for a while!"

"Well, you thought right," Rose giggled.

Rose handed her card to the cast member scanning the Fast-Passes, and

William followed suit. Not very long after, they arrived at the beginning of the ride. William entered the boat-themed vehicle first, so that Rose would not have too much trouble getting out of the ride once it was over.

"Wow! That was beautiful!" Rose squealed.

"What was your favorite part? Mine was the scene where you were flying over Big Ben in London."

"Mine was where we were flying over all the mermaids."

After a few more rides, they had another bite to eat near the Haunted Mansion, where Rose once again ate a ton of food to fill her stomach and the baby's as well. Soon, they were done eating and headed towards the Haunted Mansion ride. As Rose and William entered the front gates of the ride, grim grinning ghosts sang along the line. As they snaked through the line, Rose began to grow nervous.

"WELCOME FOOLISH MORTALS TO THE HAUNTED MANSION!" The ghost host bellowed.

One painting on the wall went from a normal-looking portrait of a man into a rotten-looking painting of a decomposing corpse.

"Please make your way into the gallery," Said the ghost host.

"Everyone move into the center of the room and fill in all the… dead space."

"Hmmmm," The ghost host chuckled.

Rose grabbed William's hand and held it tightly. William looked into Rose's eyes and said reassuringly, "It's fine, it's just a ride."

The walls began to stretch as everyone looked around at the four very different pictures. One was a young girl with brown hair, holding an umbrella. The next was an older man with a brown beard and a black suit. Another was a man with a top hat, bushy sideburns, and a dark brown suit. Finally, there was a kind-looking old lady with brown hair tied into a bun. She was also holding a rose.

"Is this haunted room actually stretching or is it your imagination? Hmmmm…" The ghost host said, as the walls stretched taller and taller."

The portraits began to stretch as well, revealing the true meaning of the painting. The young girl's portrait grew into a girl on a high wire above a hungry crocodile with razor-sharp teeth. The next was the sad man in the black suit. He was now wearing red and white striped underwear, and socks, as he sat on a barrel of dynamite with a candle above to light the rope connected to the barrel.

Next to him was the man with the top hat and bushy sideburns. He was sitting on the shoulders of an old man with a blond mustache, and blond hair slicked to the side. The old man was wearing a faded red suit with a beige vest and a black bowtie. That man was also sitting on another man's shoulders with a black suit, brown hair combed over to the left and right, and sideburns that connected to a bushy beard at the end of his chin. He was the last man in the tower of very different looking men.

Next to the very bottom man was a sign that read: "QUICKSAND," and was exactly where the sign and the tower of multiple men were stuck. The kind-looking old lady began to look very suspicious when she was sitting on a grave with a stone replica of a man with a unique mustache and an axe that was buried in the man's bald head. The grave read: "REST IN PEACE, DEAR BELOVED GEORGE."

"As you can see, this chamber has no windows… and no doors."

"Which gives you this chilling CHALLENGE!

"TO FIND… A WAY OUT!

"Muahahahaha!" Said the ghost host.

Rose held William's hand even tighter.

"Geez, my hand is gonna be red when this ride is over!" Said William, starting to laugh a little.

"Sorry, I'm just scared," Rose said, leaning into William.

"Well… there's always my way…"

The lights suddenly went out, and a clap of thunder and a flash of lightning came from the ceiling. Everyone in the room looked up. A man was hanging from an old rope, with lightning flashing through the windows that surrounded him. A lady screamed as the lights came back on, and the ceiling returned to its former look.

"I didn't mean to frighten you prematurely," the eerie voice said.

"The real chills come later… now as they say, look… alive."

As Rose and William walked down a dark hallway lined with paintings, they noticed that the paintings would change into a darker, more decrepit scenes, when the lightning flashed through the windows. Rose and William eventually made it to the Doom Buggies. The ride slowly and gradually made its way up a stairway that led to a never-ending hallway. A few more eerie scenes and a few minutes later, they made their way to the graveyard.

About halfway through the graveyard, Rose and William noticed a strangely out-of-place coffin. The lid was open to the left, leaving the interior of the coffin exposed to the elements.

When the safety bar was raised, Rose and William began to walk back to the castle.

"Uh, I don't feel so good..." Rose moaned.

"Did the ride make you dizzy or something?" William asked.

"I don't know, but I think we should go," Rose said, beginning to have pains in her stomach.

"But the fireworks are about to begin. We can't miss those!"

"Wait… okay, I think I feel a bit better," Rose said, still holding her stomach as the pains died down.

They began walking towards the castle. A few minutes later, the speakers announced that the fireworks were about to begin in just a few short minutes.

As they entered Main Street, William said, "Just in time," smiling broadly while staring at the castle lit up with multiple colors.

A few short minutes later, the show began. A firework that looked like a shooting star shot over the castle, as a boy began to sing:

"Star light, star bright, first star I see tonight, I wish I may, I wish I might, have this wish I wish tonight."

"Wait, Will, we need to go, NOW!" Rose shouted.

"What? What's wrong?" asked William.

"It's coming! And I'm not kidding this time!"

Rose began to scream in pain as fireworks burst over the castle. She began to breathe heavily.

"Okay, let's get you to a hospital. Just stay calm," William said, trying to notify a cast member to help them to the front gates to leave.

A few cast members noticed William shouting for help and Rose screaming in pain.

"Can you help us get through the crowd? My wife is about to have our baby!" William shouted, as the people around him began to stare even more than they already were.

"No, we have to get you in somewhere close by, your wife could have the baby any second now," the cast member said.

"There!" The cast member pointed at the castle.

Rose began screaming even louder.

"Okay!" William shouted, as he picked up Rose and carried her into the castle.

The cast member closed the curtains they used for shows and called a nurse from the first aid center to come help deliver the baby. With the curtains closed, more fireworks burst into brilliant, beautiful colors in the sky. A few minutes later, the nurse rushed to the back of the castle and into the corridor where the cast member, Rose and William were.

The nurse, her hair tied up in a ponytail, was wearing a white medical jacket and baby blue scrubs. She kept her white jacket open so that guests could see the Disneyland cast member name tag that read: "Betty."

Betty ran into the gift shop and grabbed a few shirts. She also grabbed a bag to put the shirts into to make a pillow for Rose's head. Betty then grabbed a Disneyland blanket for Rose to lay on.

There were pallets against the wall that held various props. Betty and a cast member cleared one and pulled it onto the floor. William sat Rose on it as she began to scream again.

The nurse began to count down.

"3, 2, 1, push!"

A few minutes later, right as the baby was born, the nurse announced, "It's a boy!"

As soon as she said that, he began to cry. At that moment, all the power on Main Street went out. The crowd of people enjoying the fireworks show gasped, and a handful screamed. As the baby let out another cry, a shooting star shot over the castle that glowed blue and left a glittery yellow trail resembling pixie dust. But the shooting star was not just another firework that Disney used for the shows. It was... the WISHING STAR.

Chapter 3

As the nurse handed Rose the baby, Rose began to tear up. William kneeled down to get a better look at the baby. The baby had bright green eyes and dark brown hair with chubby cheeks.

"What should we name the little fella?" William asked, thinking of a name.

"Exton, his name is Exton," Rose said smiling.

William looked at Rose and nodded with a smile.

"OH!" Rose shouted in pain as the nurse took the baby from her. "Something... something's not right..." Rose said, grabbing her stomach again.

A group of paramedics rushed into the castle with a stretcher, and picked up Rose and laid her on it. They also took the baby from the nurse and wrapped him in a blanket, and then handed him to Rose.

As the paramedics began leaving the castle, William grabbed one by the shoulder and asked, "Where are you taking my wife?"

"To the hospital. Disney notified us that a baby was being born on the premises, so we were dispatched right way to help as fast as we could," the paramedic said, as William let go of the man's shoulder.

They rushed Rose down the path leading out of the castle, with William following. Once they got Rose and Exton down the darkened Main Street, the paramedics cleared the street.

People in the street made their way into the shops or onto the sidewalk. As the baby opened his eyes and looked up at Rose, the lights came back on Main Street, lighting the way out of the park. It brought a huge smile to everyone in the crowd. Not too much longer, the paramedics, Rose, Exton, and William made their way to the ambulance.

As the paramedics picked up the stretcher and moved it into the back of the ambulance, William jumped into the back as well. Rose let out another cry of pain, trying to keep it low, so that she wouldn't scare Exton. The paramedics closed the back doors after a woman paramedic jumped in to hook Rose up to the IV bag. She also strapped the stretcher down to the ambulance, so that it wouldn't move around as they drove away.

The female paramedic opened the window to the driver and gave him a thumbs up, so that he knew it was safe to start driving. A few minutes later, they made it to the hospital that was closest to Disneyland.

They wheeled the stretcher Rose and Exton were on out of the ambulance and into the hospital. The nurse unraveled all the wires that Rose was connected to, and hung them on the IV pole that was rolled along with the patient.

William jumped out of the ambulance after the nurse and ran up to Rose, as a policeman pushed him back.

"Sorry, you can't go down this hallway without a pass, or unless we're instructed by a nurse or doctor that you can go with your wife," said the bulky police officer with a gold badge that read: "Officer Mike."

William pushed the man against the wall and ran up to Rose. The policeman followed after William, grabbed him, and started to say, "Sir…"

The nurse cut him off.

"He's okay. Let him in."

The policeman let William go, as William shrugged his shoulders and straightened his shirt. They made their way up to the 13th floor of the building and transferred Rose from the stretcher to a bed in the room. Rose let out another scream from the pain. A nurse began to take Exton, but Rose stopped her.

"I will always love you..." Rose kissed sleeping Exton's forehead as tears fell down her face.

Rose grabbed the back of her necklace, pulled it over her head, and gently put it over the baby's head and onto his neck. She gave Exton one last kiss, as the nurse took the baby out of her arms and placed him in a smaller version of the stretcher, except it had no belts to buckle the baby down. It also had a glass case surrounding the sides of it, and no top so that it was easy to take the baby out of it.

"Where are you taking our child?" William asked.

"To the nursery," the nurse said.

As Rose let out another scream, the baby began to cry once more. When Exton cried, the glass on the edges began to crack up the sides and into the corners. He let out another cry, as the nurse rolled him to the nursery, and the lights began to flicker in the hallway. The nurse looked up at the lights and heard Rose let out another scream, as she continued to roll Exton down the blue painted hallways and into the nursery.

Back in the hospital room, Rose's body was drenched in sweat. As William held Rose's hand, she began to speak.

"Will... Thank you for taking me to Disneyland. It was already the happiest place on earth, but this trip has made it even happier. I love you."

William began to cry as he gave her a kiss on the hand. Hearing loud footsteps, William turned around. Several doctors burst through the door. He only remembered one doctor that turned toward him and his name tag read: "Dr. Munden."

"Everything will be fine, sir," the doctor said.

The same policeman followed in after them and grabbed William, pulling him towards the door. William tried to break free from the man, but he was too strong for William to handle.

"ROSE!" William shouted, still trying to break free from the man.

Rose let out one more shout as her heart rate began to drop, and the doctors began rushing around even more than they already were.

The policeman finally managed to get William out of the room. William tried multiple times to open the door again and again, but it just wouldn't budge because the door locked from the inside. He decided to give up on this futile act, and just sat on the bench across from the room, hoping beyond hope that Rose would be fine.

All of a sudden, he heard the heart rate completely drop as it began to emit a long beep. William ran up to the door and began to bang on it with his fist over and over, as he cried perilously. His fist desperately banging on the door began to have longer beats between each strike. He collapsed onto the floor not long after.

When the doctors came out to tell William the devastating news, he was gone. He had already started walking down the blue painted hallways, with the lights still flickering, to get his son.

As he knocked on the nursery door for the nurse to let him in, she was holding Exton, feeding him. The look on William's face said it all. The nurse turned around and grabbed a baby cart, moving it toward William. She then laid the baby down in it and rolled the baby cart to William. William carefully picked Exton up and cradled him in his arms. William walked down the glossy floors with the lights still flickering. He stopped at Rose's room, placed his hand on the door, and with tears falling down his face, William said, "Goodbye, my love."

12 Years Later

Beep, Beep, Beep. Exton looked at his alarm clock. It read 7:30 a.m. Exton sat up on the side of his bed in his Superman sleeping pants, and rubbed his eyes. With the clock still beeping, he reached over to hit the alarm clock, but he missed and hit his phone.

As it lit up, the calendar flashed March 16. Exton's eyes opened wide, as he rushed into his closet and threw his clothes on. With the clock still beeping, he barely opened up the closet door and threw his navy blue Vans at the clock.

Exton had now grown into a very handsome young man, with dark brown hair, bright green eyes, and a very strong jawline like his father. As Exton made his way down the stairs, the smell of coffee and pancakes began to grow stronger with every step he took toward the kitchen.

"Hey, Dad!" Said Exton, as he grabbed a pancake from the stack and set it down on a plate that was already laid out for him.

"So, are you excited for tomorrow?

It's your birthday!"

"Yeah, but it reminds me of mom. I miss her even though I barely knew her for three minutes." Exton laughed a little, but he was crying on the inside.

William tried to keep a straight face to teach his son to be strong, so he held it in.

"Well, off to school we go!" William said happily, trying to change the subject.

As they both got into the car, William said, "Forgot the keys!" and went back inside to find them.

"This is like the seventh time, Dad, geez," Exton said, yelling at the half-open window.

As Exton sat in the car waiting for his father to return, a picture of his mother fell from the car's sun visor and landed in his lap. It was the Polaroid picture taken of his mother in front of the castle. As he began to cry a bit, a tear fell from his chin and hit the top left corner of the picture. To Exton, it resembled a firework bursting over the castle. As he began to cry even more, he heard the doorknob shake. Exton wiped his tears with his shirtsleeve. It was a plain blue shirt, and he was wearing blue jeans and black Converse, with his dark brown hair combed to the side.

Exton did not have enough time to put the picture back in the sun visor before William returned to the car. He quickly placed it in the side of his backpack, where he usually kept a water bottle. As William got into the car and started it up, Exton hoped that his father wouldn't notice the picture was missing. A few minutes later, they reached the final stoplight before Exton's school.

"Don't be afraid of the bullies," William told Exton, looking at him then back to the stoplight, waiting for it to turn green.

"Stand up for yourself. Don't let them push you around anymore," William said.

"But what if I get in trouble?" Asked Exton.

"Trust me. I'll get you out of it. But that doesn't mean fight them, you know. Well, unless you have to," William said, as he laughed and lightly punched Exton in the shoulder.

Finally, they were at the front of the line of cars letting their children out. "Hey, remember what I said!" William said pointing at Exton.

"Okay, Dad, I'll be fine," Exton said, closing the car door as William drove away.

Exton walked into school not very confident in himself, as usual. He walked into the main part of the building with the grand staircase to the second story classes, the entrance hall to all the electives, and finally, a massive stage for school plays and musicals.

The school day was going well until third period. Exton was walking to science class, but he was a few minutes late due to issues in math class. As he walked down the hall, he noticed three bullies skipping class. He tried to pass them by holding his binder up to his head, but that wasn't enough. The three eighth graders noticed him and decided to give him a little talk.

The main one knocked the binder out of his hands and pushed him against the lockers on the left side of the hallway. The main bully was named Luke; he was also the captain of the football team. He always wore sporty clothes with tall socks, and his hair was a bit darker than Exton's. It was also very short with just a little height in the front.

The other two were both blond. One had long hair, and the other's was a bit shorter hair with brunet roots. They also both wore sporty clothes.

"I'm not afraid of you," Exton said with just a bit of pride in himself.

"Well, you should be!" Luke said laughing, as he gave his friend with the long blond hair a fist bump.

Luke punched Exton on the left side of his jaw, and he collapsed to the floor. He then picked up Exton's backpack and started looking through it. Exton tried to stand up. The shorter blond-haired kid, kicked Exton in the stomach and he fell back down.

Luke pulled out the picture of his mother and said, "Aw, look, the little baby still needs his mommy."

The whole group laughed as Exton pulled himself up, still coughing.

"But wait, I thought your mom was Maleficent?" Luke said laughing.

"What?" Exton asked confused.

"Well, you look a lot like her. You have her jawline and cheekbones. But just not her powers. What a shame," Luke said, faking a sad face.

Luke ripped the picture of Exton's mother in half right in front of him.

"NO!" Exton shouted.

"What are you gonna do?" Luke asked, laughing dramatically.

This has gone on way too long, Exton thought to himself.

He also remembered what his father said, "I said, what are you gonna do?"

Exton kicked Luke in the chest into the middle of the hallway, he began to lean over and cough. The other two backed up a little, because they could see the hate in Exton's eyes.

Luke picked himself back up and said, "You little…"

Exton shot out a green bolt of lightning like energy, and it pushed Luke into the lockers, leaving his shape in the locker as he slid onto the floor. Exton looked at his hands in fear, then looked back up at Luke.

"You truly are the son of Maleficent," Luke said, as he coughed one more time before saying, "Malefison!"

Exton ran out of the hallway in complete fear. Every step he took left a crack in the ground that got bigger and bigger, until it reached the wall and onto the ceiling. Big, thorny roots began to grow out of the walls and floor, as the ground began to crack even more. The ceiling began to fall as well. It almost caught up to Exton, but he got out just in time.

He made his way into the main room. The thorns had beat him there, and the stage was completely destroyed with the curtain ripped to shreds. The cracks in the ground rumbled behind and under him, leading to one of the many pillars holding up the room. The crack finally reached it, and the entire ceiling came crashing down with even more pillars crumbling with it.

Exton ran faster than ever to the entrance of the building. He ran out on to a patch of grass in front of the school that was a good distance from the destruction. The building soon became swallowed in thorns, as the cracks reached the front of the building. Exton ran away and didn't turn back to see the final destruction of the school.

Chapter 4

Exton ran to the sidewalk on the side of the street near the school entrance. When he began to run in the opposite direction of the school, he heard the tumultuous sound of stone smashing on the concrete. As he turned around to witness the damage, the smoke and dust from all the broken bricks and stone began to clear. The front of the school building was completely destroyed.

Thorns were still growing from the broken windows and cracked walls. He noticed his classmates and other students, who he only recognized from the hallways, running out of the part of the building where his powers had not yet reached.

As everyone ran to the fence a good distance away from the school, the cracks and thorns made their way to the only part of the building that was left. A few moments later, all that was left was debris and rubble from the broken bricks and stone on the outside of the building. People began driving into the school's parking lot to see what had happened. Exton ran in fear into the woods across from the school, hoping no one had seen what he was capable of.

As he made his way into the woods, Exton's hands started to twitch as the ground began to shake. He ran to the closest tree and backed up against it. Even more thorns began to grow in front of Exton's eyes. They got closer and closer to Exton as he backed up, hoping they would stop soon. As he was backing up, he didn't notice the stone in the dirt, and tripped on a branch, knocking himself out.

Meanwhile, his father was at work and received a call that the school had been completely destroyed. William instantly panicked and rushed to the school. When he got there, all the smoke had dissipated. Now, all the damage was visible.

William parked his car in a parking space close to the edge of the woods. He got out and walked up to a group of kids and a number of teachers. A nurse was on the side helping anyone who had been severely hurt. The only kid who seemed majorly hurt was Luke. He had a bandage around his left arm and right leg. Luke didn't tell anyone about Exton because he was too terrified that it would backfire somehow.

William walked up to a teacher who was in her fifties, with salt and pepper hair, wearing a red vest and a dark gray skirt. The teacher was counting.

"Thirty-six, thirty-seven, thirty…"

"Do you know where my son, Exton, is?" William asked, cutting off the teacher.

"No, sorry! Go talk to the principal. He's over there talking to all the parents."

As William walked up to the crowd of parents, he started to hear their questions get louder and louder about what happened at the school. William knew that he would never get the chance to ask where his son was.

He walked up to the crowd of kids and yelled out, "Exton!"

He was hoping that Exton would walk out merrily and healthy, but he didn't walk out at all. Police were still on their way to search through the debris, but William didn't have the patience. He walked over to where the school entrance used to be and saw something shining in the middle of the debris. William stepped onto the rubble and carefully began to walk over to the shiny object. He knew that if Rose was here, she would tell him that he was going to break his ankle or something, but Exton was all he had left.

Dodging the thorns, William made his way to the shiny object successfully without breaking his ankle. The shiny object was a button of Mickey Mouse on a backpack.

He began searching again, and then he noticed he had bought that same pin for Exton on a trip to Disneyland. William reached to grab it from under some rubble, but it was stuck to something. He cleared the stone and pieces of metal out of the way. It was Exton's backpack.

William cleared more rubble, hoping Exton was not still attached to the backpack under the debris, letting out a sigh of relief when he realized it was only his backpack. He picked it up and dusted it off.

He also noticed something lodged under another piece of stone. It was a larger stone, so William used all the muscle he had to pick up the stone and throw it aside. It was the picture William had taken of Rose but ripped in half.

Wasn't this picture in my car? William thought to himself.

And even if a stone fell on it, it would be damaged but not ripped in half like this. William wondered what could have done this. He put the two pieces in his pocket.

William kept searching, but there was no sign of Exton, and he began to panic. He ran back to the group of kids and shouted, "Exton!" one more time. There was still no response.

The police soon arrived, as William was still looking for Exton. They approached William and told him to leave the premises, and that if they found something or someone, they would notify him. William wrote down his number on a small notepad that one policeman had in his pocket. As William walked back to the car, the thought of losing his son was killing him.

On the way home, William was stuck in traffic due to an accident half a mile down the road. All his memories of with Exton began to play back in his head, just as they did when Rose passed away.

After about two and a half hours, William still had not received the call that Exton had been found in the damaged school. The search team had not found anything in the wreckage, so they began to look outside the school, wondering if any kids were outside when it took place and ran home or into the woods.

Back in the woods, where Exton had hit his head and was knocked unconscious, he was just waking from his slumber. He looked around because he had forgotten where he was, but not how he had gotten there. As his eyes began to focus on the dark oak trees, he was no longer surrounded by the fearsome dark thorns. He was laying on a patch of leaves, grass, and flowers. The rock that he had landed on had somehow settled into the ground. Exton's head was no longer laying on it; he was resting on a soft patch in the grass. The edge of his naturalistic bed was a row of thick pointy thorns, pointing outwards into the woods. Exton realized that his power tried to destroy him, but it also tried to protect him.

While Exton was still looking at his surroundings and had recovered most of his memory, he heard footsteps approaching. He jumped up in consternation, fearing someone had found him. He ran behind a bush close to the sound.

A group of policemen had been searching in the woods. He immediately thought they were after him. Exton ran out of the woods as quickly and as quietly as he could. He made his way back to school property, and turned around to see if he had been followed. There was no sign of them. There was also no sign of the students or any of the teachers.

As Exton's foot touched the school property line, something clicked inside him. All the regrets, the worries, the questions about how he got these powers, what he was going to do with them, and how he was going to control himself, flooded him. Exton didn't want to lose his father; he had already lost his mother. He didn't want to kill or even hurt his father with these powers he knew nothing about.

The word "Disneyland" and the date, "March 17," replayed in his head over and over. Exton stopped in his steps and gasped. He suddenly remembered that he had been born in the Sleeping Beauty Castle at Disneyland on March 17th. Not only was March 17th Saint Patrick's Day, a stroke of good fortune, but what else could have occurred on this day? He knew where he needed to go.

Exton ran into the damage and rubble, hoping he could find his backpack. He had earlier memorized the map of the school to find a way around Luke if he needed to. That considerably helped him to find his way to where he was last, before the building collapsed.

Exton made his way to where the backpack should have been. He knew he was in the right area because there was a locker on the ground with a Luke-sized dent in it. Yet, no backpack was to be found. Exton immediately thought of his father, and rushed down the sidewalk, towards the street.

Exton's house was not too far from his school, but there was a highway in between. He made his way to the street, trying to stay as tranquil as he could while running, so as not to draw attention to himself.

He made it halfway down the street and almost to his neighborhood when his hands began to twitch again. Frantically, he began to run faster, hoping to get home before his powers manifested. All of a sudden, the sound of cars honking at each other began to grow louder. He began to see the flashing lights of a police vehicle not too far in the distance. He also heard sirens at close range. He slowed down when he got closer to whatever it was.

Exton had finally made his way around the turn to witness a car, hood first, in a ditch. He couldn't see what was happening for a few seconds because of the cars passing in front of him. But, there was one car that stood out from the others. It was his father's.

He knew it was his dad's because of the Mickey Mouse antenna topper on the car. Once he noticed that, he began to run once again. He didn't turn around to look for his father; he was petrified that something would happen.

A few minutes later, Exton finally made his way home. Overwrought with his legs throbbing and aching, he ran into the garage, picked up the welcome mat, and grabbed the key beneath it. He briskly ran into the living room and up the stairs to his bedroom to get some black clothes. He promptly snatched a pair of black Nikes, black jogger pants, and a black Spandex sports shirt. He grabbed a black hoodie just in case it got a little chilly outside. He also seized his mother's necklace off the dresser next to his bed.

As he slipped the necklace over his head, he heard a car door shut. Exton hurdled over his bed and opened one of the blinds to peek out. It was his dad.

Exton grew apprehensive. While putting his shoes on vigorously, he heard the garage door creek, and thought to himself, *Did I forget to shut the door?*

He instantly made his way down the stairs. He noticed his backpack had been placed down near the garage door. Exton took a quick look around to make sure his father was not there, before running over and promptly slipping it on.

He was almost out the door when he remembered that Disneyland was further away than his school. He ran back into the kitchen and began to open the cabinets on the island, hoping to find a bus pass. He was out of luck. It was not there. As he tiptoed to his father's room to look in the nightstand, he began to hear footsteps. Luckily, there was a closet not far from the bedroom.

He quickly hid inside it, hoping to be obscured. Only a bit of light was visible inside the closet, coming through the crack at the bottom of the door. He waited, hoping to hear the footsteps grow faint, but he heard the steps on the wooden staircase.

He immediately opened the door and darted into the bedroom. He began to search in the right side of the dresser. Still no luck; all he found was some old reading glasses, a flashlight, and some books. He walked to the other dresser on the left side near the bathroom and began to search. He found the bus pass and a season ticket to the park.

As he turned his head to put the tickets in his bag, he noticed his father standing there, and he jumped.

"What are you doing here? I was worried sick!" William said, hugging Exton like the python in the jungle book.

"Umm… I ran away right before the building collapsed," Exton said, stuffing the tickets in the water holder part of his bag, as the Disneyland ticket slipped out.

"But how did it collapse?" William asked, letting go of his son from the long python-like hug.

"Trust me, Dad, I wanna know just as much as you.

"Well, I gotta get going," Exton said, as he began to walk towards the door.

"Whoa, whoa, whoa! Where are you going?" William asked, as he stopped Exton by grabbing him by the wrist.

"Oh, I was just going to spend the night at a friend's house," Exton replied.

"Not to be nosey or anything but… have you made a new friend?" William asked.

"Yeah, I ran into him the other day while switching classes."

"Oh, okay!" William said with a sad look on his face.

"What's wrong?"

"Nothing. I was just thinking we could go to out to eat or something for your birthday," William replied.

"Dad, my birthday isn't until tomorrow."

Exton tried to hide the bus pass with his palm.

"Well, okay, I guess I'll see you tomorrow morning then?"

"Yeah, for sure!" Exton said walking out of the door, as his hands began to twitch.

"Okay, bye!" William said, trying to sound happy for Exton.

As William closed the dresser Exton left open, he noticed a Disneyland season pass for one. When he slipped the ticket back in, he realized that one of the bus passes was missing. After such a trying day, he decided not to give it much thought.

Chapter 5

As Exton walked into the garage, he made sure to turn around and close the door. He walked to the left wall in the garage and grabbed his bike off a bike rack that hung on the wall. As he placed the bike on the concrete floor, he noticed the tires were as flat as the Kansas plains.

Exton walked over to the built-in cabinets, opened one of the doors, and pulled out the tire pump. He connected the pump to the tire and pulled the handle up. As he pushed the handle down unknowingly with vigorous strength, it went way too far and cracked the pump in half.

"Oh my gosh!" Exton said frantically, backing up into the countertop that was mounted against the wall.

Wait, Exton stopped and thought to himself. *First the thorns, now this!*

Okay, thorns equal Maleficent? I guess strength equals Hercules? Exton gasped, wondering if he got those powers from that shooting star.

"Heh, look at me talking to myself in my head," Exton said out loud.

"No, you're not alone. I was listening to you," a voice in Exton's head said to him.

The voice sounded like a girl about his own age.

"Wait, what! Who are you?" Exton asked to the voice looking around the room.

"That's not important at this time. What's important is getting you to where you belong!" the voice said.

"And where exactly is that?"

"I thought you already knew that!" The voice said to Exton.

Exton could sense that the voice had a smirk while saying that to him.

"Yeah, right!" Exton said to the voice in his head.

"Then I guess you'd better get going!" The voice replied.

"Yeah… guess I should…"

"Wait! I almost forgot!" the voice said.

"Close your eyes," the voice commanded of Exton.

"Okay!" Exton said as he closed his eyes.

"Now… think happy thoughts," The voice commanded again.

"Okay!" Exton said to the voice, thinking of spending his birthday with his mom.

"Now… Open your eyes," the voice said.

When Exton opened his eyes, he was hovering over his bike and broken tire pump. Exton gasped just as he hit his head on the ceiling.

"Ouch!" Exton yelled, closing his eyes as he rubbed his head, not really knowing what was going on. He then opened his eyes and said, "Wait! What!?"

Exton started wiggling and his arms started flapping, as if gravity had been turned back on.

"Oooh, I felt that one. Sorry, Exton," the voice said.

"Wait... How do you know my name?" Exton asked the voice.

"Oh, trust me, I know all. I can also see all," the voice said.

"What are you?" Exton asked.

"You'll find that out soon enough."

A few minutes later, the voice persuaded Exton to fly again. It took a while to get out of the garage, but he did it and landed softly on the concrete.

"Okay, let's try this one more time. We have to get you to the bus station!" the voice said to Exton.

"Okay, here I…"

Exton began to float upwards until he commanded himself to stop in his mind.

"Go!" Exton said, as he immediately began to fly through the air.

He went slowly at first, but as he progressed, he began to go faster.

"Okay! I see the bus station!" Exton exclaimed.

"Okay! Remember everything I taught you! Lean down, then fly back up a bit!" the voice instructed Exton.

There was no reply from Exton.

"Exton?" The voice shouted.

Exton's face was buried in a tree with a few leaves sticking out of his hair.

"I'm okay…" Exton muttered under his breath.

"Seriously, are you okay?"

"Yes, I just got the wind knocked out of me."

"Whoa, I almost thought you got hurt there." The voice chuckled as Exton tried to lower himself from the branch he was holding onto after the impact.

As the branch began to crack, Exton said, "Should have taken the bike…"

The branch snapped, sending Exton hurdling towards a pile of leaves. "Ahhh!" Exton screamed, as he landed in a pile of leaves behind the bus station.

The leaves didn't break his fall very well, but it was better than nothing. Exton stood up as he brushed the leaves off his hoodie and pulled the leaves out of his hair. He noticed the bus coming down the road; it let out a big "eek" as it came to a stop. The doors opened as the LED sign on the front of the bus changed to "Disneyland Resort."

As Exton boarded the bus, the driver stopped him and asked, "Where are your parents, kid?"

"Oh, they're waiting for me at the entrance of the park. So, can you please hurry?"

"Okay, geez, sorry to bother you, kid."

"Sorry, I'm just in a huge hurry," Exton said.

"No worries, kid. Can I see your bus pass, please?"

Exton pulled out his bus pass from the side of his backpack and handed it to the bus driver. The man turned around and did something to the card, but Exton couldn't see from where he was standing. A few seconds later, he handed Exton his bus pass.

Exton took a seat close to the front so he could get out faster, even though no one was on the bus besides him and the bus driver. The driver swiftly closed the bus doors, and the bus progressed down the road. Before long, they were only a few minutes away from the resort.

"Hey, if you don't mind me asking, why aren't you in school, kid?" The bus driver asked Exton, looking at him in the review mirror.

"We got off early for spring break," Exton replied. Technically, that was true, except the school was kinda destroyed.

"Oh, okay, cool," the bus driver laughed.

"And one more question."

"Hm?" Exton seemed annoyed.

"Why are you going to Disneyland by yourself?"

"Oh, remember… I'm meeting up with the rest of my family."

"Okay, well, we're here kid." The bus came to a creaking stop, and the driver pulled hard on the lever to open the door.

As Exton walked down the stairs, taking his first step on Disney property, the man shouted, "Have fun!"

Exton made it down the bus station pathway and to the entrance of the resort. Walking down the pathway with huge crowds of families entering the resort, the smell of hot dogs and churros grew stronger with every step he took towards the entrance of the Magic Kingdom.

To the left of him was the California Adventure Park. Exton wasn't born there. He was born in the heart of the Magic Kingdom. As Exton walked near the gate of the park, a monorail zoomed by on the track above his head. Exton looked up, as he turned around and began to walk backwards.

He then heard the train whistle blow "Toot, toot!" As he turned around, he came face-to-face with a beautiful girl. She had bright blue eyes, dark brown hair, and was wearing a colorful T-shirt that had a silhouette of Minnie Mouse's head on the front, with the words, "Never Stop Dreaming!"

"Oh, I'm so sorry. Did I hurt you? Are you okay?" Exton asked the girl as they both took a step back.

"No, I'm totally fine," the girl replied.

"What's your name? I'm Exton."

The girl's eyes opened very wide as a smile formed on her lips.

"Wait. Aren't you the person who was born here when a shooting star passed over?" the girl asked as if she was quickly trying to change the subject.

But Exton didn't care. All he cared about was that he was talking to the most beautiful girl he had ever seen.

"Um… yeah, but how exactly did you know that?"

Chapter 5

"That story is still known today. I'm sure everyone knows that story," the girl replied.

"I guess it was a pretty big deal."

"Yeah, and I know how it felt to lose your mother. I lost my father.

"Wait... How did you know that I lost my mother? I know for a fact that was not in the story. My father didn't want any more grief." Exton said.

The girl looked petrified. "I guess I know more of your story than others do," the girl said, casting her eyes downward.

When Exton turned around to reach for his ticket to the park, the ticket was gone, and the girl was gone as well. "What the?" Exton thought.

"Hey, see that crowd of people entering the park?" The voice was back with more to say.

This time, however, the voice sounded very like the girl he had just met.

But Exton didn't care to think much of it. "Yeah, why?" Exton replied to the voice.

"Duck down and get in the middle and try to pass as one of their family members," the voice said to Exton.

"But I don't have a ticket," Exton replied.

"I know. Just stay down and try to squeeze through with them," the voice said.

"Ooh! Okay, got it."

Exton ducked down and walked into the group of people entering together. When Exton reached the cast member scanning the tickets, he was stopped for his own ticket.

"Oh, I'm with that family that just walked through. Didn't my mom just scan my ticket?"

"Oh, yes, are you... Braxton?" the cast member asked.

"Yup, that's me, Braxton!" Exton said nervously.

"Okay, then, I guess you're in! Have a magical day!" the cast member said.

"Thanks," Exton replied.

Exton made his way through the turnstile and into the park. Suddenly, he saw the Mickey Mouse made out of flowers and couldn't help but smile.

Exton entered the Magic Kingdom under the train station, in a tunnel that showed various Disney shows, rides, and more. He walked down the street and into the middle of Main Street, USA. As he looked at the castle, he tried to remember what happened during his birth that could have given him his powers. Then, he remembered once again that he was born inside the Sleeping Beauty Castle just as a shooting star shot over it.

Exton ran down Main Street and up to the Walt Disney statue. As he stepped onto the bricks placed on the ground, one was loose, wobbly, and even a bit higher than the others.

Not very many people were in the statue area at the time, so Exton felt comfortable enough to go and pick it up. As he touched the brick, his eyes opened very wide. He witnessed every recollection he had stored in his mind of his mother. It was being played in some kind of weird slideshow inside his mind. He could see the sparkling gleam in her eyes and hear her infectious laugh.

When the strange slideshow finally finished, Exton had more memories of his mother than he could ever have imagined. Exton fell back, but luckily caught himself on the iron bars around the statue. Breathing heavily and sweating profusely, it was obvious he didn't want to touch that brick again, but he had to see what was underneath it. He bent back down and reached towards the brick, poking it very quickly to see what would happen. But nothing did happen. He then carefully picked up the brick.

Underneath was some sort of treasure chest, with the words: "Laughter is *timeless,* Imagination has no *age,* and Dreams are *forever.*" All around the top was a dark-green thorn pattern.

Exton read the words on the box aloud, as the box suddenly flew open. The box began to rattle and shake, as he struggled to close it. When he did so, the box let out a bolt of energy that struck him in the heart. Exton finally closed the box with all his might.

People began to walk towards the section he was in, so he quickly unzipped his backpack and slid the box inside. He thought it could possibly come in handy. He then quickly got up and walked off, as if nothing had happened.

As Exton walked through the Sleeping Beauty Castle, he was hit with massive emotions of consternation, and uneasiness mixed with anxiety. Then all of a sudden, Exton's eyes opened very wide, and his pupils dilated greatly. He had just gotten hit with even more memories of his mother and his father in the stretching room pre-show of the Haunted Mansion. Suddenly, he became befuddled, because he hadn't even been born yet. Exton's pupils shrunk to normal size after the flashes of quick memories were over — a clairvoyant moment. He knew he had to go into that ride to see what had happened there, and if it had anything to do with his powers.

As Exton walked into Fantasyland, his heart started to ache, but he didn't think much of it. The buildings were bright and colorful as always in Fantasyland and full of love. But he had to go to the darkest part of Disneyland, so he began to walk.

Exton took a left towards Frontierland and Big Thunder Mountain Railroad. Big Thunder Mountain Railroad was a runaway mine train ride that took you through twists and turns and in and out of caves. The ride had two peaks and looked like a mountain in the Old West. When he walked towards the big ride, a runaway mine train came shooting out of a cave and hurdled down around the old mountain bend. Exton jumped as it happened.

A few minutes later, as he entered the New Orleans Square section, he heard a big clap of thunder. Shaking slightly, he looked up, as did everyone else near him. There was a dark cloud surrounding the park, with small flashes of heat lightning scattered within it. As the cloud began to drop water down onto the pavement around the park, visitors fled into the closest buildings. Exton was very close to the Haunted Mansion, so he made a run for it.

As he entered the gates to the Haunted Mansion, the rain fell even harder, as a bolt of lightning struck the top of the mansion. Terror stricken, Exton jumped and slipped, hitting his head on the concrete. For what seemed like an eternity, he just lay there, drenched in the rain.

Finally, a few cast members walked over to help him to safety. Trying his best to focus, his eyes began to flutter, until he finally just passed out.

Chapter 6

A few hours passed before Exton woke from his deep slumber. He tried to open his eyes but closed them a few times to adjust to the light. Exton sat up and looked around the room.

He was lying on a gray exam table with paper rolled over it, like being at the doctor's office for a check-up or a flu shot. As he began to sit up, a young-looking lady walked through the door to the room.

"Hi, my name is Scarlet Jones. I'm the Nurse Practitioner here at Magic Kingdom."

Exton fully opened his eyes and began to rub his head. The first thing Exton noticed was that she had beautiful dark-brown wavy hair.

Scarlet was holding a clipboard with a few notes jotted down on it. She was wearing a white lab coat that had a pocket on the front embroidered with a black Mickey Mouse head. Under the coat was a fancy blue skirt that was sewn onto a top of the same color. On her feet, she wore a pair of black dress shoes. Still trying to recover, Exton didn't reply to the woman.

"It's a miracle you didn't go into a coma," Scarlet said, clicking her pen as she wrote something down on her clipboard.

"If you don't mind me asking, where are your parents?"

Exton tried to think of a lie, but when he got one, he wasn't able to say anything.

"Okay, I guess I will just check on you later and let you recover. Bye for now!" she said, as she walked out the door and closed it.

Exton had a very bad feeling about that doctor. He didn't know why, but he just felt negative energy. He rubbed his eyes to wake himself up even more. He sprang off the bed, trying not to make a sound. Unfortunately, he slipped and kicked the metal trashcan, which made a loud ringing noise. Exton stopped in his tracks and waited a moment to see if anyone had heard the noise. No one had walked in the door, so Exton continued with what he was doing. He immediately grabbed his backpack and put it on. The bag began to glow green through the zippers, and it started to shake. Before Exton could take the magical box out of his backpack, it pulled him into the left wall. The magic rested for a few seconds, then slammed Exton into the right wall, with a huge thud.

Exton heard footsteps coming towards the room. He looked around for a way out, but there was no exit. As the doorknob began to twist, the bag flung Exton up into the air and onto the ceiling.

Scarlet Jones walked into the room once again to find that Exton was gone. He looked down at her from the ceiling, hoping she would not notice him. Deftly, Scarlet pulled out her phone and began to dial a number. She raised it up to her ear and began to speak, as she walked away and closed the door. Exton immediately plummeted down onto the cold tiled floor.

When he got up, he walked towards the door. As he opened it, he inconspicuously poked his head out to make sure that no one was there. When he walked down the hall, he heard the woman speaking on the phone in room number 13.

Exton pressed his ear against the door to hear what was going on.

"I don't know where he went. Send out security to find him. We can't let him get away or expose his powers to anyone. Whatever the cost, get him back, or we will have to pay it."

When she was done, she hung up, not allowing the other person to talk, whoever or whatever it was.

When Exton heard her high-heeled shoes clicking on the tiles, he quickly ran into the room next to her office. Once there, he barely cracked the door open so he could see if it was safe to leave. As Scarlet made her way outside the building at the end of the hall, Exton darted towards her office. He quickly closed the door and locked it, wanting to find some clues as to what was going on. As he began to look around through piles of books and papers, he came across a cabinet labeled, "The Lucky One."

Exton opened the cabinet, wondering what he would find, and what he found was astonishing. It was his mother's death record, but there was something odd about it. It was only filled out halfway, as if the person signing it just stopped or even disappeared. Another peculiar thing that he found was the same exact Polaroid picture of his mother in front of the castle.

"What the…" Exton said, pulling out more and more papers and stacking them on top of each other.

The most disturbing part of all was finding his own birth records, with the necklace his mother gave him taped to the front. Exton looked down at his chest to see that it was gone.

She must have taken it while I was unconscious, Exton thought to himself.

Exton pulled off the necklace and slipped it over his head. When he walked over to Scarlet's desk, there was a manila folder sitting on it. Exton took off his backpack, unzipped it, and then snatched up the folder and slid it in underneath the box. When he put the backpack back on and stood up, Scarlet was standing there looking at him.

"What are you doing in here?" Scarlet demanded.

"Oh, um… about that…" Exton said, as he darted around Scarlet and out of the room. .

"Hey, get back here!" She yelled.

When Exton was nearly out, Scarlet shrieked, "Get him!"

Two large security guards came bombarding into the room. Exton pushed his hands out in front of him, sending the two grown men flying.

"He already knows! He knows too much!" Scarlet yelled.

Exton exited the building and re-entered Main Street. He began to run towards the exit of the park, but decided to take a sudden right into the Disneyland fire department building.

Exton walked to the wall on the side of the building that had a door that read: "CAST MEMBERS ONLY." He began to force the door open, until he realized it was unlocked. Exton walked into the backstage area and up a ramp that led to Walt Disney's private apartment.

When Exton walked into the apartment, which was Walt Disney's home away from home, he sensed cigarette smoke, but it was very faint. It had been resting in the room for over four decades now.

Exton looked around the room. The Victorian details were exquisite, with a wooden Regina music box set against the wall. Exton walked towards the window. Sitting on a desk was a very famous lamp, which represented the presence of Walt Disney watching over the park to this day. Exton pulled the curtain back and looked out the window. Scarlet was nowhere to be seen.

He felt very at home in this building, and he was not sure why. He even felt a sense of déjà vu, a hint of melancholy, as if he had been here in this very room several times, but maybe not in this lifetime. Exton needed to rest. He sat down on a white-flowered printed chair. When he took off his backpack, the Regina music box began to play. Exton felt petrified. He frantically stood up and grabbed his bag; he wanted to leave as soon as he could.

As the darkness of the night fell, the candle sitting on the desk glowed brighter and brighter. The music box was so soothing and calm, he began to feel sleepy. He sat back down in the white rose pattern chair. He slipped his backpack off and let it slide to the floor. The lamp acted as a soothing night light for him. Exton fell into a deep slumber, napping as if he was back in that moment in 1955.

Exton awoke to total silence. The music box had stopped playing, and the silence was deafening. Exton sat up and rubbed his eyes, and walked towards the window. He carefully pulled the curtain back, and looked out the window. Main Street was entirely empty, not a soul to be seen. Exton fished out his phone and checked the time.

"11:58 p.m.," The clock read.

"Wait! What!?" Exton exclaimed, as he grabbed his backpack and sprinted towards the door.

He slung the door open and fled down the ramp leading towards Main Street. Every step he took on the ramp made a loud thump. Exton ran to the gates under the train station. They were closed and locked. Suddenly, he was trapped in the happiest place on earth.

He began to panic, and started breathing heavily and running his fingers through his hair. He walked into the middle of the street and slowly turned around. He stared at the clock on the train station: "11:59."

The sweep hand on the clock only had five seconds until it reached 12 midnight.

"Tick, tock, tick, tock, tick…"

The sweep hand clicked as it struck twelve. Then the clock let out a loud tock, as Exton's heart ached even worse than last time. The anguish stopped very soon.

Suddenly, a thought came to Exton. *Wait, it's my birthday! I'm thirteen!* Exton smiled to himself.

"Well, I guess I'm locked in here now," Exton said aloud, as he pulled out his phone to call his dad.

As Exton's first finger was placed onto the screen, it began to wig out, and then shock him. He immediately dropped the phone, watching it shatter into several pieces on the pavement.

"Oh, that's just perfect! Now I don't have any contact with my dad or anyone!"

Maybe now that I'm thirteen, my powers are gone, or maybe I'm even more powerful now, Exton thought to himself.

Exton stuck out his hands. As he did so, a bush of thorns began to grow on a plot of grass, with flowers attached to the train station stairway.

"Same old thing, nothing different!" Exton said, as he turned towards the castle.

All of a sudden, he heard a strange sound behind him. He slowly shifted his head around bewildered. The thorns on the plot of grass had become a beautiful rose bush, and bright green vines grew down the side of the concrete wall, holding the plot of grass. The vines had white and red roses on them. Exton was very proud of himself, until the vines kept growing and began growing faster and faster.

He began to run down Main Street towards the castle. He spun around and stuck out his hands to try to stop it. But it didn't work. An invisible force of energy shot from his hands, sending him flying multiple feet in mid-air.

When he stood up, the girl that he had met earlier that day was standing in front of him, with her hands outstretched towards the wild vines. A blue, sparkling energy was being forced from the girl's hands and onto the vines. The vines began to stop growing, then finally shriveled up and died. The girl dusted off her hands and extended her right hand out to help Exton up.

"Hi! I'm Alana!"

Exton declined her help, as he scampered back, and then got up.

"What? Are you scared of me now, or something?" Alana asked.

Exton had no reply.

"Hello! Exton?" Alana said, as she waved into his dead face.

"How do you know my name?" Exton asked under his breath, kind of fearful of her response.

"I told you I see everything, and I also know everything."

Exton waited a few seconds in shock, then said, "You're the voice in my head!"

"Yup."

"I thought I was crazy or something!" Exton replied very happily.

"Well…" Alana said, as she giggled.

"Come on, I wanna show you something." Alana began to run towards a "Cast Members Only" area on Main Street.

"Umm… Do you have a key or what?" Exton asked.

"No, but watch this!" She grabbed Exton's hand and shut her eyes, as she whispered some sort of spell.

"FROM THE PRESENT

TO THE PAST,

WE LEAVE YOU AT LAST,

OFF WE GO,

TO WHAT ONLY WE KNOW!"

When Exton blinked, he was standing inside the legendary Lilly Belle caboose!

"No way!" Exton said.

"Yes, way!" Alana replied in a flash.

Exton and Rose were standing inside the legendary Lilly Belle, a train caboose named after Walt Disney's mother, and which was only used for VIPs.

"Ever wonder why the cart was only used for VIPs?" Alana inquired.

"Isn't it because the cart was very old and they didn't want it damaged or something?"

"No! I found out that Disney had the first time machine," Alana said.

"What do you mean?" Exton asked.

"I mean once Walt Disney lost his mother, he used every bit of magic to try to bring her back, but he couldn't. So, he brought himself back to the time when she was alive."

"Wow," Exton said.

"Yeah, I know. Sit down, watch this," Alana said, as the creaky old train wheels began to move, sending them down the train tracks.

"Okay, hold on to something! Here we go."

Exton looked around. He couldn't find anything on the antique caboose to hold on to, so he just decided to sit next to Alana and hold her hand.

"Is it okay if I just hold your hand instead?" Exton asked Alana nervously.

"Um… sure…" Alana said smiling, as her cheeks reddened. He didn't mean anything by it, but he was completely fine with holding such a beautiful girl's hand. The cart began to rock and shake, as it sped down the tracks, faster and faster. As they passed in front of the Disneyland train station, the cart was accelerating to massive speeds.

"Ahhhh!" Exton screamed as Alana just laughed at him.

A blue swirl started to surround the cart as it progressed down the tracks, until it finally engulfed it. The swirl was shades of dark blue, light blue, and light purple. The train seemed to slow down while in this worm hole.

It felt safe enough in the cart to stand up and walk around. Exton stood up and walked towards the front of the cart, and looked out the window. As it was coming to a stop, a giant gold stopwatch with a train on its cover appeared in front of the train. When the stopwatch opened, its chain grabbed the train and started pulling it closer. Exton began to step back. Alana was completely still, just watching Exton.

The train stopped once again, as the chain unraveled. The numbers on the watch began to fade, as it became another sort of worm hole with flashes of illuminating lights, and one tiny speck of light aglow at the end of the tunnel.

"Might wanna hold on for this one…" Alana said.

Before Exton could find a safe place to hold onto, the cart accelerated to the highest of speeds, faster than the Rock 'n' Roller Coaster at Walt Disney World Resort in Orlando Florida.

He was launched to the back of the caboose. Exton's scream echoed through the worm hole. As the light came closer and closer, it became brilliant. Everything around them became nothing but white light.

Chapter 7

When the bright light dimmed, the car was moving slowly and safely on what looked like the Disneyland railroad track.

"Wait… Are we back where we started?" Exton asked.

"No, look around. What do you see?"

Exton walked over to the window. When he looked out, all he could see was construction of what seemed to be Disneyland. The Sleeping Beauty Castle was all gray and had no color. The ground was mostly dirt. Crushed limestone was being installed, leveled, and compacted for the asphalt to be laid.

The Main Street buildings were just now starting to be built, with multiple pieces of wood laying around. To the left, you could see an orange grove being cleared. A man was standing in the middle of the street, talking to construction workers.

This man had slicked back hair and wore a fancy suit.

"No... way!" Exton said, as he turned his head towards Alana.

Alana nodded her head at Exton.

"Walt Disney!" Exton jumped with enthusiasm.

"Are we going to meet him?" "No, unfortunately!" Alana said.

"Why not? He's literally right there!"

"Well, if we get off, we won't have a way back through the portal," Alana said to Exton, as his happiness turned to sadness.

"Well, I guess that makes sense," Exton said, as he looked back out the window with a somber face, as if they had just passed the ice cream shop.

Alana stood up and walked over to Exton.

"We should get going now…" All at once, the caboose began to shake and rattle. They both looked out the window at the same time.

The construction of the park began to grow more rapidly.

"What the?" He whispered under his breath.

Everything was now in fast-forward. The park seemed to be completed, as people flooded through the gates. Then all of a sudden, it was the 10th Anniversary of Disneyland. Then the 20th, 30th, 40th, 50th, and finally, the 60th Anniversary of Disneyland.

Exton and Alana were mesmerized, with what they had just witnessed. They were right back to where they had started. The entire existence of the Disneyland

Resort had just flashed in front of Exton's eyes.

"Come on, I have something else to show you."

A few minutes later, Exton found himself at Club 33 in New Orleans Square.

"Come on!" Alana said, as she darted into the building.

When Exton entered, he was dazzled with the magnificent staircase and elevator.

"Follow me!" Alana said, as she ran into the elevator.

When the doors closed, she began to type in a code on the keypad. As she did so, a slot opened up behind the buttons.

"I found this not too long ago, and I still have no clue what it is," Alana remarked, pointing to the clover-shaped slot in the elevator.

"Wait... That's the shape of my necklace," Exton said excitedly.

Exton pulled the necklace over his head and placed it in the slot. A green light flashed behind the necklace, as the elevator "dinged." When the elevator doors opened, they were in some sort of peculiar office. On each side of the walls were windows, yet something was strange about them. They had no view, just dirt behind them. One window had a hole in it due to a tree root barging its way through. In the middle of the room was a custom-built dark wood table. At the end of the table was the tallest chair. This chair had the shape of Mickey Mouse's head on the very top. In fact, on this Mickey Mouse head, was a very bold "W" sitting over the top of it.

Just as they stepped out of the elevator, Alana heard footsteps coming from somewhere in the room, but she couldn't figure out from where.

"Wait... Exton! I hear footsteps!

Hide!"

They each hid behind a chair. Exton was having an anxiety attack, while Alana honestly wasn't frightened of the woman. When they peered around the sides of the chairs, the footsteps suddenly stopped.

As Exton looked around, he spotted Scarlet guarding the elevator. Exton gasped, as Alana turned to see what the fuss was all about.

"Who are you?" Alana asked.

"I think the real question here, girl… is who are…" Scarlet started to reply, but Exton cut her off.

"Scarlet, Scarlet Jones." Exton smiled, as the lady became enraged.

"Shut it, kid! Scarlet smirked. "You're all coming with me."

"No, we're not," Alana barked.

"It seems like Alana is taking more control now, if you ask me," Exton said in his head.

"You know I can still hear you, right?" Alana pointed out, as she turned towards Exton.

"I don't know what you're talking about, but get up and come with me. NOW!" Scarlet shouted.

Exton and Alana both stood up and walked towards Scarlet. Scarlet pulled out her phone and began to speak to someone again.

"I finally got them. Meet me at Club 33."

As she began to walk towards the elevator with Exton and Alana, Alana yelled, "NOW!", as she pushed Scarlet away from them.

"Oh, you're gonna regret that, kid!" Scarlet said, as she walked towards Exton.

He stuck out his hands and pushed her into the elevator with his powers. Alana quickly ran up to the elevator, closed the iron gate on it, and used her magic to lock it.

"Let me out now!" Scarlet demanded.

"Come on, we gotta find a way out!" He began to wildly look around.

"Found something!"

Alana started pulling a painting away from a wall that was attached with hinges.

Exton ran over to the painting. It led to a small hall. At the end of this hall was a door that had green light glowing through it.

"Come on!"

Alana leapt through the doorway, with Exton following her.

"Don't go in there! Something bad will happen!" Scarlet cried.

Exton opened the door for Alana, and as she entered, he followed.

"Whoa... Where are we?" Exton asked.

"To be completely honest, I really have no clue."

They were standing in a room that had glass display cases with wood edges. Inside these cases were what seemed to be magic wands.

"Are these what I think they are?" Exton asked.

"I think they are…"

As they kept looking around, Exton stumbled upon one case that was attached to the wall. Inside this case was a wand that was completely black, except for a brown leather handle near the bottom. At the bottom was a bright green crystal, and above the case was a brass plaque labeled: "Malefison."

Exton was very confused, but he knew that this wand was meant for him.

"Hey, Alana, come over here. Look what I found."

"Whoa! Did you just get your own magic wand?" Alana marveled. "So jealous!" Alana said laughing.

Exton opened the case up and took the wand out of the velvet holder. He began to wave it around.

"Hey! Be careful with that thing. We don't know what it does!"

Just then, a green bolt of energy instantaneously shot out of the wand. As it did so, the green crystal lit up. The energy bounced around the room, as Exton and Alana jumped and ducked, so it would not hit them. The energy finally calmed down.

"We should get going before you destroy something, like your school again," Alana said, as she walked towards the door at the other end of the room.

"Wait, how did you even know about that?"

"Do I have to say it again Exton? I'm a Gypsy. I know all and I see all."

Alana pulled a small crystal ball out of her pocket.

"Wait, Exton, look!"

As he looked into the small crystal ball, two grown men were entering the building of Club 33.

"Come on! We have to go!" Alana said, as she put the ball back into her pocket.

Alana opened the door in shock.

"What the heck!" Alana said astonished.

The door led to absolutely nothing at all. All that was there was a wall of dirt with pebbles and roots.

"Exton, see if your wand does anything!"

Exton waved his wand, then pointed it at the door. Alana closed her eyes tight and plugged her ears. The crystal glowed bright green once again, as a gateway appeared.

"Come on!" Alana cried, as she scampered through.

Exton was not so sure about this, but he followed. Soon, Exton and Alana were on the pirate ship in the lake surrounding Tom Sawyer's Island, which occasionally hosted "Fantasmic."

"Come on! We need to hide before they find us again."

"Oh, in here!" Exton said, walking towards the captain's quarters.

Exton opened the old pirate door, only to be surprised by a room full of beautiful gems, gold, silver, and reales.

He placed his wand in his back pocket, to have an extra hand to look at all the loot. He began to move his hand towards the pile of gold coins. As he stuck his hand in, he was surprised that it was all artificial, just simply plastic.

"Ow," Exton said, as he rubbed his hand from the pain of punching solid plastic.

"Did you seriously not know that was fake? Come on, Exton, seriously," Alana said mockingly.

"Oooh! Look at this!"

Exton went over to a plastic skeleton sitting in the chair behind the desk. When he went to touch the too real looking skeleton, Alana reacted.

"Okay, that might just be real... Don't touch that..."

Exton immediately took his hand away from the prop.

"Just kidding!" Alana started laughing hysterically.

"Hey! We need to be quiet. We are the only ones left in the park. They might just hear us!"

Exton took the skeleton off the chair and placed his backpack on the floor. He sat in the custom-built leather chair with wooden edges designed to look like waves. At the top of the headrest was a skull and crossbones.

"Hey, can I see that wand for a second? I wanna check it out." Alana was clearly enjoying herself.

"Wait, I found something weird..."

The green crystal seemed to be a bit loose. When Exton tugged on it, the crystal popped right out of the slot.

"I might've broken it," Exton said, sheepishly, handing Alana the two pieces.

"What? No, let me see…"

All of a sudden, the small crystal ball inside Alana's pocket began to blink. Alana barely noticed the light out of the corner of her eye. She took the ball out and placed it on the desk to examine it. The ball rolled right into the slot on the wand and snapped in place.

"Hmm, that's weird," Exton observed. "Wait, let me see that."

As Alana handed the wand back to Exton, he tried to pull the ball out but failed.

"Hey, let me try."

Exton handed the wand back to Alana, who was able to pull the crystal ball out right away.

"Maybe only I can pull my source of power out of the wand and place it in there," Exton said in awe.

"That might just be it!" Alana placed the crystal ball back in.

"Can I go try this outside?" Alana asked.

"Sure, why not? But we need to be super careful not to get caught."

Exton got up from the chair and walked with Alana to the door.

"Okay, shh…" Alana whispered as she opened the door to darkness, and felt a cold breeze on her skin.

Alana stepped out towards the edge of the ship and delicately waved the magic wand. As the crystal ball glowed a bright brilliant blue, the water in the lake began to rise. Alana waved the wand like a conductor, as the water shot in different directions and even changed colors.

Back on the other side of the lake, Scarlet and her goons had escaped. "Hey, I see them! Let's go!" one of the goons said.

"Wait, wait, wait! Let them get their hopes up. Then, we will get them when they least expect it," Scarlet said, as she chuckled with pure evilness.

"Hey, watch this!" Alana said, as a fountain of water shot out of the lake and launched towards Exton, but he managed to dodge it.

"Hey, don't do that!" Exton said laughing.

"Fine."

Alana waved the wand just one more time.

Multiple fountains of water shot towards Exton once again.

Exton dodged almost every single one, but was hit by the last. He looked at Alana with a startled face, trying not to laugh.

"Oh, I see how it is!"

Exton stuck his hand out towards the lake and launched a huge ball of water towards Alana. She quickly swung into action, waved the wand, and then directed it at Exton.

"Okay, time!" Exton said, as Alana stopped the ball of water hurdling towards Exton.

"Ha! Ha! I win!" Alana boasted and they both laughed.

"Okay, I think it's time you learn where you came from," Alana said.

"Okay, now I'm not having that talk again."

"What? No, no, no, I mean where your POWERS are from!"

"Oh, okay, good!" Exton felt relieved and laughed as well.

As Exton and Alana walked back inside, she told him to sit in the chair.

Exton did so, and Alana sat on the table.

"First of all, do you know how you got your magic?" Alana asked.

"Yes, I was born inside Sleeping Beauty's Castle, as the Wishing Star passed over," Exton said proudly.

"Yes, but that's not all. Your mom was a descendant."

"Of whom?" Exton looked bewildered.

Alana spoke the words slowly, "Walter Elias Disney."

Chapter 8

"Did I just hear that right?"

"I don't know, did you?"

"So, you're telling me that I'm related to Walt Disney?" Exton seemed shocked.

"Yes."

Exton exerted joy, as he spun himself around in the chair.

"Whoa, whoa, whoa, slow down. If you had magic like me, it wouldn't be as enhanced. But you came from a line of Disney's! You have the same bloodline as the most imaginative man in history!" Alana boasted proudly.

"But this comes with big responsibilities. You have to learn how to control your powers."

Exton heard a loud clank, coming from further down in the ship.

"Did you just hear that?" Exton looked puzzled. He pulled out his wand and stood up.

"No."

Exton heard another loud clank.

"Okay, I heard that one," Alana confirmed.

"Shh! Stay behind me." Exton quietly tiptoed towards the door.

The door creaked, as Exton opened it very slowly. Exton peeked around the corner and looked around the ship to make sure no one had followed them.

"Coast is clear on deck."

"Okay, I'm gonna go down to the cargo area. You stay here," Exton advised Alana.

"No! I'm coming with you."

"To be completely honest, I was hoping you were gonna say that."

As they made it through the ship, it was quiet, almost too quiet. The sound of a few barrels falling over, startled them, as they walked through the cold dark room. The wooden planks creaked with every step. Exton got as far as he could with no light. Then, he began to wave the wand to light up the room. All of a sudden, two red lights lit up in the darkness, then two more.

"What are those?" Alana asked.

"I don't know. Get behind me!"

The first figure began to walk towards Exton. It soon stopped in its tracks. It got quiet too fast. Then all of a sudden, the figure launched into action. Baring its teeth at Exton, it began to attack him. The figure was an old rusted pirate animatronic. It had ripped clothes that showed its rusted, broken endoskeleton. The head of the animatronic was a rusted metal skull, with gleaming metal teeth. One side of the skull had a hole in it that exposed the red and yellow wires. Bizarrely, this animatronic wasn't connected to anything; it was controlling itself! Then two more animatronics appeared that were very similar to the first one.

When Exton began to wave his wand, one of the animatronics knocked it right out of his hand. As he bent to pick it up, the pirate skeleton let out a loud ear-piercing scream.

All of a sudden, the clanking of more animatronic footsteps came from behind them. When they spun around, to their surprise, a weathered Jack Sparrow walked out into the light.

His hair was much more tangled than in the Pirates of the Caribbean ride. Jack seemed to have lost his hat, but the bandana was still resting on his cold metal skull, with a layer of silicone skin. His white shirt had a large tear in the middle, and so did the skin, revealing his thin robot-like skeleton, much like the skeleton pirates. His blue vest seemed to be just fine, except for a few spotty stains from an unknown substance. Jack Sparrow reached for his sword and unsheathed it with flair, as it shimmered in the weak blue moonlight.

"Let's go!" Exton directed, as he and Alana sprinted up the stairs and onto the deck.

All was calm for a few seconds.

"Maybe they can't walk up stairs," Alana said.

Jack Sparrow and his pirate crew emerged from the darkness.

"Three a.m., m, m, m, m," Jack Sparrow repeated, due to a short in his system.

"Three a.m., the time we awake, fellas!" Jack said, as his Pirate posse cackled.

"Who are you?" Exton shouted towards the animatronics, hoping they had some sort of system to answer questions.

"I think it's more of a what than a who, mate," Jack sputtered.

"You know, 3 a.m. is the most evil part of the night? Well, in our case, it's our day. At this hour, we do what we want and where we want!" Jack threw back his tattered head and swung up his sword.

"We're not scared of you!" Exton shot back. He turned around to find Alana had run away.

"Come on now, REALLY!" Exton's frustration mounted, as Jack began to walk forward.

"Stand back!" Exton cried out, but Jack just laughed and kept walking.

"I said 'STAND BACK!'" Exton tensed with anger.

"Come on now, mate. I just wanna have some fun until it's time for me to go!" Jack muttered.

He swung his sword at Exton, who swiftly dodged it. Jack soon swiped down again, this time at Exton's ankle, cutting through his pants right above his shoe. Exton screamed in pain from the laceration and collapsed onto the wooden floorboards.

"Our night's just beginning, but I think yours is pretty much over!" Jack bellowed.

He raised his sword, ready to end Exton's life. Exton shut his eyes in despair. Then, out of the blue, he heard all of the skeleton pirates fall to the ground. Jack turned his head completely around, and his body turned shortly after. Alana was standing beside a pile of rusty robots. In her hand was the wand with her crystal ball inside.

"Ah! Alana… So glad to see you so soon again." Jack gallantly smiled at Alana.

Exton was still incapacitated from pain. He tried to stand up but failed.

"Let him go now! I'm not here to start a conversation with you, Jack!" Alana pointed the wand towards him with determination. Exton finally gained the strength to stand up.

"Exton, here!"

Alana let out a high-pitched screech, as she pulled out her crystal ball and tossed the wand to Exton. He swiftly caught it in mid-air.

"This, too!" Alana shouted.

She tossed the green crystal to him. She barely missed him, and it bounced off the side of the ship and landed in the lake.

"Ah, tough luck!" Jack grinned and let out a fake sigh.

Exton quickly used supernatural magic from his hands and shot Jack forward. Jack was only pushed a few feet away, due to how heavy he was. Exton hoisted himself up onto the edge of the ship with all his might.

"Come get me, Jack!"

The pirate rotated around and ran toward Exton screaming, with his metal jaw wide open. Jack didn't run very fast, but was certainly intimidating. Every step he took with his big metal feel crashing onto the wood made the ship jolt. When Jack got close enough, Exton did a back flip with his arms out, his wand in his right hand, and landed perfectly in the deep dark water.

"Well, at least he's done with," Jack said.

Bubbles with a lime-green glow started to form in the water. From the cold lake, Exton came shooting out and flying into the air. He had the crystal in one hand, and the wand in the other.

"Well, I guess this is a Peter Pan moment," Jack said sarcastically.

Exton swooped down and shot a bolt of energy at Jack. Jack started to shake and gyrate like his short was getting the best of him. Exton shot another bolt, as Jack fell down onto his mechanical knees. Jack's black hair was dangling over his silicone face, while smoke began to emit from his body.

Exton, thinking he had won, descended down to check it out. Jack was making weird sounds, as Exton's powers surged through his metal body.

"Is he dead?" Exton asked, as he looked towards Alana.

To Exton's surprise, Jack unexpectedly jolted into action and threw his sword at Exton's wrist. Exton was then attached by the sleeve of his hoodie to the wooden spar in the middle of the ship that held the mainsails. As Jack fully sat up, his silicone face melted away, revealing a sculpted metal skeleton-like face. Exton tried to use his wand but couldn't move his wrist enough to cast a spell.

"I think our little game is over now, mate," Jack said.

Jack pulled out his old pirate gun. Alana immediately ran to the melted mechanical machine and used all the power in her body to throw him against the ledge. Exton ripped his hoodie by pulling himself off the sword.

"Now I think we're done here… mate!"

Exton picked Jack up with his wand and tossed the lifeless metal body into the lake. As the animatronic sank lower and lower, the body sparked until it finally just gave up.

"Whew!" Exton collapsed in victory. Alana bent over on her knees, laughingly nodding her head.

Exton's leg began to bleed profusely.

"I guess I didn't even notice it, with all the excitement flowing through my body." Exton propped himself against the edge of the boat.

"Let me grab something to stop the bleeding."

Alana hurried over to one of the lifeless skeleton pirates and ripped a bandana off one of them.

"Here."

Alana carefully wrapped the bandana around Exton's ankle.

"Sssss." Exton reacted in pain.

"Okay, I gotta pull this tight now. It might hurt a bit."

Alana pulled each end of the bandana and tightened it.

"AHHH!" Exton screams in pain.

"Wait, I almost forgot!"

Alana ripped the bandana off of Exton's leg.

"AH! What are you doing?" Exton reared his head back in pain.

"Just watch."

Alana placed her hands over Exton's wound and began to sing.

"Flower gleam and glow, let your power shine, make the clock reverse, bring back what once was mine... What once was mine..."

Alana stopped singing and picked up her hands. The wound on Exton's leg was gone!

"How did you do that?"

"Rapunzel's reversal spell," Alana said proudly.

"Oh, yeah, totally knew about that."

Alana giggled. "Okay, now try to stand up."

Exton shakily stood up. "Good as new! By the way, what time is it?"

"Oh, umm, let me check."

Alana pulled out her crystal ball. It began to shine. Exton leaned over to check it out. The crystal ball read: "3:11 a.m."

"Wait, isn't 3:00 a.m. the most evil part of the night?" Exton asked.

"I think it is, Exton! You might just be on to something," Alana said, as she chuckled a bit.

"And didn't the animatronics come to life at, let's say, roughly 3:00 a.m.?"

"Yeah, that sounds about right."

"Follow me. We need to check something out."

Exton began to walk toward the front of the boat. He jumped from the boat to the pathway.

"Where are we going?" Alana asked as she leapt off the boat.

"We need to go to Fantasyland." "Why?" Alana asked.

"If the animatronics just came alive, then we're gonna have a big problem in Fantasyland."

Chapter 9

Exton and Alana made their way back to Fantasyland. They both felt edgy. The lights were off in this section of the park, causing the Matterhorn Bobsleds ride to catch their eye. Exton peeked his head around Pinocchio's Daring Journey. He heard the sound of something rummaging through a trashcan. All of a sudden, it went tumbling onto the stones on the ground, causing a loud clank.

"What was that?" Alana whispered into Exton's ear.

"I don't know. Stay right here."

Exton darted towards the carousel and hid behind one of the horses. He gradually looked over the saddle of a fiberglass horse to see what was in Fantasyland with him. Finally, he noticed a large white furry creature walking around. The funny thing was it moved just like an animatronic should.

The creature released a few grunts while holding a trashcan. It then let out a horrific scream. As the scream bounced off each building and into Exton's ears, he knew where that scream came from. It was from the Yeti in the Matterhorn Bobsleds!

Exton scurried back towards Alana, who had her eyes shut tight and was holding her ears.

"Alana, we have to go now!"

Alana opened her eyes and stared above Exton. She was traumatized.

"What's wrong?"

"Look…" Alana's face went white as she pointed behind him.

Exton knew exactly what was behind him. He could feel the cold air breathing down his neck.

He did not want to turn around, but something inside him made him turn anyway. Exton stared into the Yeti's eyes, hoping his confidence would make the Yeti not notice him. The Yeti was still standing there with his red glowing eyes staring directly at him. Alana snapped her fingers as the carousel began to light up and spin.

"Come on. He's distracted. Let's go!"

Together in one swift movement, they darted towards the castle. The sound of their footsteps on the ground caught the Yeti's attention. He let out another ear-piercing scream, as he launched towards Exton and Alana.

"Stand right here beside me. On three, jump out of the way," Exton commanded, as he stood in front of a skinny pillar that was holding up the back of the castle.

"Are you CRAZY?" Alana roared, as she stood beside Exton.

"ONE... TWO..." Exton counted down, as the Yeti was only a few feet away at this point.

"THREE!" Exton shouted, as he and Alana jumped in opposite directions.

The Yeti tried to stop itself, but it was too late; he was running too fast. The Yeti slammed into the pillar, causing part of the castle balcony to give way and come crashing down onto the mechanical beast. Its red eyes began to flicker and fade away from its cold, blue face.

"Wow..." Alana said.

"What?" Exton looked confused.

"I just realized why Disney has such a good cleaning crew!" Alana ran her fingers through her hair and began to crack up.

"Yeah, I guess." Exton laughed as well.

"We should take a break from all this fighting and do something fun. I mean, we are at Disneyland!"

"Yeah! Seems like a good idea to me." Exton began to smile.

"Wanna ride Snow White's Scary

Adventures?"

"But none of the rides are working," Alana said.

"Here, watch this."

Exton stuck out his hand and waved it from the left side of Fantasyland, then to the right. The lights began to illuminate, but something wasn't right. It was too quiet. Usually the crowd during the day filled the void of the quietness. But it wasn't just the quietness bothering Exton. He felt something there with him and Alana. The rides began to operate without anyone having to work them.

"Did you do that?"

"No, I just turned on the lights," Exton said, looking around at the rides.

"I guess we can ride Snow White now."

"Okay, let's go," Exton said.

The window where the Evil Queen looked out was open, yet the Evil Queen was gone. Exton just ignored it, knowing that Disney was doing a few renovations. Exton and Alana began to get in a mine cart. The one that had been selected was the Dopey mine cart.

"Ha, I guess we got Dopey because you trip and hit your head so much!" Alana said laughing.

"Yeah, I guess," Exton said, rubbing his head and giggling.

As the ride began by entering the Seven Dwarfs' cottage, the music playing was the sound of birds chirping and the dwarfs singing, but all the animatronics had seemed to have vanished.

"Where are Snow White and the Seven Dwarfs?" Alana asked, examining the room for the animatronics.

"Wait, if the Yeti was alive… Then, shouldn't these animatronics be alive?"

As they left the cottage, they could hear the Evil Queen talking. They were staring at the spot where she is usually supposed to be. As they entered the Seven Dwarfs' mine section of the ride, they began to even wonder why they decided to get on a ride in the first place.

The gems and diamonds were glowing in magnificent colors. Various shades of brilliant blues, greens, vivid purples, and radiant reds flooded the mine. However, this still couldn't lighten the mood of fear. The mine came to an end, as they approached the Evil Queen's castle. Big wooden dungeon doors opened as they entered the Evil Queen's lair. It didn't seem as though the Queen had been in this scene either.

The mine cart came to a halt in front of the Evil Queen's Magic Mirror.

"Is this part of the ride?" Alana asked, looking slightly worried.

"If it is, I don't remember it."

The Magic Mirror begins to crack.

"Um… Exton… is this an illusion?" Alana asked, as she pointed at the mirror.

"Come on! We have to get out!"

Exton used his strength to bend the lap bar.

"Come on! We have to go."

Exton grabbed Alana's hand and helped her out of the cart. The mirror shattered into multiple pieces, which were propelled through the air towards them. Exton covered Alana, as they both closed their eyes. When the shards of glass had finally stopped flying, they both stood up and looked at the mirror with allurement.

The mirror seemed to open up to some kind of dark room. A hazy figure began to walk towards the opening of the mirror. Exton pulled out his wand, getting ready to fight.

"Get behind me," Exton ordered Alana, and she did what he said.

The Evil Queen stepped out of the Magic Mirror. She moved just like the other animatronics did, but she was more fluid and smooth with an enchanting air about her.

"Oh, I don't want to fight. I am here to help you," the Queen said in a trenchant tone.

"Why would you want to help me?" Exton asked.

"Because, you and I are not that different, you know," the Queen said to Exton as she stepped closer.

"How are we anything alike?" Exton asked, challenging her.

"Well, to start, we have both lost someone we loved truly."

The Queen placed her finger on Exton's wand and pushed it down.

"We also have a deep anger and hate for someone that has ruined our lives," the Queen said.

"I don't have a hate for anyone," Exton said.

"Oh, really? Then what was this about you destroying your own school? Your anger got the best of you, Exton."

"What? Wait, how do you know my name?"

Exton pulled his wand back up and aimed it at the Evil Queen.

"My mirror tells me everything I want to hear. Well, except the time it told me I was not the fairest of them all." The Queen made a mock frown.

"Well, it got that one right, didn't it?"

Exton said, as Alana giggled in the back.

"SHUT your mouth! I was, and always will be, the fairest of them all!"

"Well, even if it was wrong, it's broken now, so you can't even use it!"

"Hm…" The Queen shifted back, as her eyes fell to the floor.

She waved her hand at the glass shards and used her sorcery to hover them in mid-air. Then, she began to form all the shards back together by ringing her hands together tighter and tighter. When the glass was back to its former shape, she pointed her hand towards the Magic Mirror and entombed the glass back into its rightful spot.

"Now, where were we?" The Evil Queen smiled.

"Oh yes! MAGIC MIRROR ON THE WALL, WHO IS EXTON, AFTER ALL?"

Then at once, the mirror began to glow. A face began to appear that resembled a theater mask.

"Malefison," the Magic Mirror replied.

"Malefison, as in the son of Maleficent?" The Queen asked the Magic Mirror.

"Yes, my lady! The son of Maleficent!" the mirror said.

As the face began to fade away, the Evil Queen turned and looked at Exton.

"Son of Maleficent, eh?" The Queen asked.

She stepped down the stairs and walked towards him and Alana.

"I'm not the son of Maleficent!" Exton shouted.

The crystal in the wand began to glow.

"Maybe not in this life, but your soul is old, very old. In each one of your lives, you were not able to defeat your enemies. Don't you want to accomplish that for once?" The Queen gave a defiant stare.

"Don't listen to her, Exton!" Alana cautioned.

"This does not involve you, Alana," the Queen said.

Exton stood totally still, thinking about what he should do next.

"Exton, please believe me! You can't listen to her!" Alana said, pulling Exton back.

"What did I just say!" The Queen shouted.

She used her magic to place Alana back into the cart. The lap bar slowly bent back into place and then bent further and to hold Alana in. The cart slowly began to proceed to the ride.

"Exton, NO!" Alana screamed, as she turned the corner, her voice getting fainter and fainter.

"I will give you the power to defeat your enemies, but I'm going to have to be in my real, physical self to do it. So you are going to help me manifest." The Queen smiled, studying Exton closely.

"What is it that you need?"

"I am going to need my magic box. It's hidden in the Central Plaza," the Queen demanded.

"Oh, you mean this?"

Exton gently placed his backpack on the floor, unzipped it, and pulled out the Queen's magic box.

"Yes, that is it!"

The Queen took the box out of Exton's hands.

"This is the box I was planning to put that Snow White's heart in, but my huntsman failed me. I'm sure you know the story."

"But why doesn't it have a heart on it with a sword through it? To me, it just looks like some old wooden box." Exton kept his eyes on the Queen.

"Oh, yes, I placed a spell on it so that no one could tell if they happened to find it. Clearly, it seemed to work because you had no clue that it belonged to me."

"Well, may I ask this? How are you even real? How is any of this even real? I thought you and everyone else were just stories on a page."

"That is just it. Walt Disney had more power than you and I combined. He made his stories come to life when he made Disneyland. But not all characters had a body to possess," the Queen said.

Exton had a confused look on his face.

"You see, Maleficent is not here, because she did not have an animatronic to control. But luckily, Walt Disney and the Disney Imagineers created one for me, much like the others." The Queen took a step back.

"Ah, I understand," Exton said.

"Yes. Now, if you don't have any more questions, let's continue what we were doing, shall we?" The Queen placed her hand over the box.

A purple mist began to swirl around the mystical box, as she spun her hand around it. When the purple mist began to dissipate, it revealed a red box with a sword through a gold heart.

"What you are going to do is open the box and stare deep inside."

"Are you sure that's it?" Exton asked.

"Oh, one more thing! Stand in front of the mirror while you are doing this."

Exton nodded and walked towards the Magic Mirror. He felt a strange, yet familiar allurement drawing him towards the mirror.

He got into position and opened the box. The box was filled with green fog, and it began to snake its way out of the box. As he stared into the green fog, it began to swirl, then quickly faded away. Suddenly, he saw his mother lying in a bed. All he could hear was beeping. He suddenly realized that this was his mother in the hospital. He felt something inside that he had never felt before.

The green fog began to rise up again, only to fade into Luke bullying him over the years, shown to him in a series of images that only flashed for a second. The feeling inside him began to grow stronger and even angrier.

The fog began to swirl once more to reveal a fire-breathing dragon that resembled Maleficent. The dragon was fighting an unknown creature, with buildings burning behind it. At that moment, Exton knew he had become that dragon. It was a symbol of his anger and hatred towards the world. He closed the box, afraid of what was next.

"Look up," the Queen said in an amused tone.

Exton raised his head up and stared into the mirror. He witnessed his eyes glowing a bright neon green, even greener than they already were.

He perceived that he was becoming a darker, angrier person. Just what the son of Maleficent would be expected to be like. He dropped the box onto the floor. It landed perfectly right-side up and opened.

The green fog was released and began to rise and swirl around him, until it finally consumed Exton's entire body.

When the fog began to clear, he stared back sharply into the mirror.

Exton was now dressed in a black shirt, a black vest, and a pair of black skinny jeans. He was also wearing black shoes with a thorn pattern on the side. To top it all off, a long black flowing cape was attached to his vest.

"I can get used to this," Exton said, looking in the mirror, grinning.

"Now, Exton..." the Queen began, as Exton cut her off.

"No...Call me Malefison."

"Well, then, Malefison, I still need your help, now that you have unlocked your true, inner power."

"What do you need help with?"

"I need you to hold my box in front of me," the Queen instructed.

Exton picked up the box and held it in front of her. The Queen carefully opened the box and stood back.

"I am also going to need you to fill the box with all your anger."

"And how do I do that?" Exton asked.

"Just hold the box on both sides and think of what you saw in the box. Your power will do the rest."

The Queen steadied herself and opened the box, as the green fog began to flow out again. Exton squeezed the box tight, as he felt the anger and hate rushing through his hands and into the box.

The green fog began to seep out and consume the Evil Queen, much like it did Exton. It swirled around the Queen's body, wrapping it in an eerie light. The green fog then faded into more of a dark purple, then a light green. The fog began to contain little flashes of light, much like a lightning storm. It began to dissipate from the top to the bottom, revealing two large, black horns. At that moment, Exton knew exactly what the Evil Queen's true form was, for the fog finally dissipated completely to reveal this.

"Well, well! I've been waiting way too long to meet you, Malefison!" Maleficent said. "And I'm pretty sure you know who I am, due to our previous conversation."

"Yes, even without our conversation, I would definitely know you," Exton said.

"Hmm, I thought so," Maleficent said, as she gave an evil smile.

Chapter 10

"**N**ow, I think you should be on your way," Maleficent said.

"Aren't you coming with me?"

"No, I have already fought my battles and failed. But that doesn't mean that I can't help you fight yours," Maleficent replied.

"How are you gonna help me fight, if you can't come with me?"

"That box didn't just change your wardrobe, Exton. It gave you what you needed. You needed to find your inner power and it seems you have. But to keep it, you are going to have to stay away from that Alana. Here, you're going to need this." Maleficent tossed the box to Exton.

"But why stay away from Alana?"

"Because, if you want to keep your true power, you cannot be with her."

"Okay!" Exton took a step back.

However, in the back of his mind, he was questioning if he had made the right decision.

A cart entered the room and stopped in front of Exton and Maleficent.

As Exton was getting into the cart, he asked, "One more thing, if you were Maleficent all along, then why were you in the Evil Queen's animatronic and acting like the Evil Queen?"

"Well, there are two reasons. The reason why I was in the Queen's animatronic is because Walt did not give me a ride with my own animatronic. So, I had to improvise and possess the Queen's animatronic. The reason I was pretending to be the Evil Queen is because I was making sure it was really you. Now, you must be on your way."

As she raised her hand up to the cart, it began to move. Exton left feeling satisfied, yet confused at the same time. As he approached the end of the ride, Alana was waiting for him at the exit.

"Exton!" Alana frantically called out.

"I've been waiting for you here!

What happened?"

Alana noticed his new look.

"She changed you, didn't she?"

He stepped out of the cart speechless.

"Just as I expected. I told you not to listen to her, yet you did!" Alana exploded in anger.

"No! She showed me who I could be and what I need to be!"

"I thought you would have come out of there good and true, but yet she changed you. She always does!"

"What do you mean, 'she always does'?" Exton asked.

"Forget it. I thought you would have believed in me," Alana said.

"No, it's just that I…"

Alana cut him off. "Save it, Exton. GO DEFEAT your enemies or something!"

"How did you know that?" Exton asked.

"Did you forget that I have a crystal ball?"

"Oh, that's right, you're a seer, psychic, clairvoyant, a fortune teller, or whatever," Exton said, rolling his eyes. "Yeah, you know what? Maybe I will go defeat my enemies!" With that, Exton ran through the castle and out onto the street.

"Exton, what are you doing?" Alana said, racing after him.

Chapter 11

Exton ran to the front of the Walt Disney statue. He placed the box in front of it and pulled out his wand. He then stepped back and pointed his wand at the box.

"Exton!" Alana shouted.

Exton shot a fluorescent green beam at the box and levitated it into the air. He raised his left hand and pointed at the statue. Walt Disney's right hand began to twist and face upwards. Exton levitated the box over to Walt's hand.

Walt Disney's fingers began to grip the box.

"Exton, don't open that box!" Alana shouted.

Exton waved the wand, as the box began to open.

"No!" Alana screamed.

The box shot a green lightning bolt into the sky. Two dark clouds began to appear on opposite sides of the bolt. They started to swirl and eventually combine into one cloud.

"Exton, what have you done?"

Everything seemed to slow down in the park, including Exton and Alana. Everything quickly returned to normal speed, as a circle of green energy burst in the middle of the bolt, much like a nuclear explosion. This resulted in a massive boom that shook the entire park. A green dome began to form around the park.

"Exton, what is this?"

Meanwhile, Scarlet and her goons had made their way into Adventureland. Scarlet looked into the sky and noticed the dome beginning to form.

"Well, he's finally done it," Scarlet proclaimed.

She pulled out her phone.

"Meet me in the Central Plaza. We found him!"

The beam let out another big boom.

"Exton, we have to stop it!"

Something suddenly switched inside Exton, and his intuition told him this wasn't right. He started walking towards the statue. The beam released yet another thundering boom, sending Exton flying a few feet back. When he landed, he switched again.

I've come too far to let my good side defeat me, Exton thought to himself.

He stood back up and walked back towards the statue. As he was walking back, he heard someone shout his name. He stopped in his tracks and looked towards the direction of the voice. Out walked Scarlet and her two goons from Adventureland.

"I've beaten you twice and I will beat you again, Scarlet!"

"You really think that we came to fight again?" Scarlet said sarcastically.

"Yes, I do Scarlet," Exton replied sneeringly.

"No, you didn't let me finish. I was going to say, did you really think that we came to fight again and not bring backup?"

Chapter 12

The sound of rustling leaves could be heard on the trees between Adventureland and Frontierland. The park rumbled with the roar of a very large creature.

"What is that?" Alana said in a petrified tone.

"I think I may have an idea," Exton answered.

As the trees came crashing down, they revealed the massive animatronic Maleficent dragon from Fantasmic. Its mechanical mouth opened up, as it let out another ground-shaking roar. It then began to breathe fire, and as the wind caught it, it was carried onto the trees around it, engulfing them in flames.

"Exton, if you're attempting to defeat Scarlet and this dragon, we're gonna have to work together!"

"No, Maleficent told me to stay away from you, Alana. You're lucky I'm even talking to you right now."

Alana stared at him with a furious expression frozen on her face.

"Exton, you're lucky I didn't just punch you.

"If we're gonna do this, we're gonna have to do this together. Please just trust me!" Alana pleaded.

"Alana, let me…"

Alana cut him off in mid-sentence. She pulled him towards her and gave him a passionate kiss. It lasted for a few seconds before they unlocked their lips. Exton stepped back speechless, gazing into Alana's eyes.

The sky generated a flashing green light. The beam began to flash as well, until it let out a green blast, then another beam, but a lighter green.

Finally, it let out a humongous bright yellow circle blast that lit up the entire Disneyland Park. It was so bright, it even caught the dragon's attention, causing it to look up.

Exton took in a deep breath.

"Alana!" Exton hugged Alana.

"I don't know what just happened, but I'm back," Exton exclaimed.

"I guess true love's kiss can break any spell," Alana said with a smirk.

The dragon once again let out another ground-shaking roar. It caught Exton and Alana off guard, as they turned and gazed at it. Scarlet had seemingly disappeared.

"Where did Scarlet go?" Exton turned to look around in all directions.

They stopped and looked down Main Street.

"This is sweet and all, but I think it's time we finish this," Scarlet interrupted.

Exton and Alana turned away from Main Street and looked towards the statue. There was Scarlet standing in front of the Partners statue with her goons.

"You know what, Scarlet?"

"What's that, Alana?"

"Never mess with a GYPSY!"

Alana pulled out her crystal ball and threw it at Scarlet. It shattered on her chest, and she began to shake before collapsing on the floor. She continued to shake until she fell over on her side, and her eyes began to dim. Scarlet's goons ran towards the exit of the park in fear.

Alana looked over at Exton. He was staring at Scarlet, his jaw dropped to the floor, and then he looked at Alana.

"What did you just do? You murdered Scarlet!"

"Okay, first of all, she was evil, and second of all, she's an animatronic. So, technically, I didn't murder anyone," Alana said defensively.

"Well, at least I know not to mess with you."

When they looked back at Scarlet, a purple energy was emanating from her body and darting towards the dragon. It then entered the dragon, who let out another horrendous scream, as now it was breathing green fire.

"I told you to stay away from that Alana!" The dragon roared, as its mechanical mouth moved up and down. "What the... Maleficent?!" Exton shouted across the plaza.

"Hahahahaha! That's right, Exton. To make sure you don't talk to that girl anymore, I am just going to have to kill her!" the Maleficent dragon snarled.

The dragon ran towards Exton and Alana with its green fire shooting out of its mouth.

"Alana, grab the box!"

Alana darted towards the statue, jumped on one of the benches, and then onto the base of the Partners statue. She reached for the box, but it was tightly secured with Walt's hand holding onto it. She tried to use her sorcery but failed.

"Exton, you distract the dragon while I get the box! Toss me the wand!"

"Catch!" Exton threw the wand to Alana.

"Hey, Maleficent! You gotta go through me first!" Exton yelled at the dragon.

"Well, if that is what you want!" Maleficent began to chase Exton.

Alana took the crystal out of the wand, and placed it in her back pocket. She reached in her other pocket for her crystal ball, but she couldn't find it.

"Oh right, duh."

Alana stuck her hand out, retrieved the shards of the crystal, and formed it back into her crystal ball. She then placed the ball into the wand. She shoved the wand between the box and Walt's hand. Alana then pulled the wand down, popped the box out, and quickly closed the box.

"Exton! Here!" Alana tossed the box to him.

He caught the box and opened it.

"Come on, come on!" He said, as the green fog began to seep out.

He ran over to the front of the castle in the middle of the compass. He threw the box onto the ground, as a dark cloud began to move towards his body. Alana raced to the back of the statue and watched Exton, as the dragon ran towards him. The dark cloud consumed Exton and began to swirl around him.

Chapter 13

As the cloud grew taller and wider, Alana looked up, following its height. The cloud stopped growing when it was almost as tall as the castle. It began to dissipate, revealing that Exton had transformed into a 60-foot fire-breathing dragon that resembled the Maleficent dragon.

The only difference was that Exton's dragon was more masculine and darker, with a dark green and purple belly, black scaly skin, and sizable horns on the top of his head.

He also had his signature glowing green eyes. His tale was about twenty feet long, and up his back were dark purple spikes that ran down his tail as well.

Alana stared at Exton in amazement. He also caught Maleficent's eye as well. Exton looked up and glowered at Maleficent from across the plaza.

To top it all, off Exton opened his gigantic wings. They were black with a dark purple outline.

"Well, well," Maleficent said.

Exton flapped his wings as he darted through the air over Alana and the plaza. He landed on Maleficent, crushing a bit of her mechanical endoskeleton, and causing barrels to roll into Main Street.

Maleficent stood back up and breathed her green fire at Exton. He got himself back up and took his stance. Exton then opened his mouth wide, exposing his razor-sharp teeth. He just sat there like that, but nothing was happening.

"Hahaha! You don't even know how to fire breathe!" Maleficent said in a mocking tone.

Exton knew exactly what he was doing. He was filling the air with gas, waiting to ignite it. He shot one green and purple fireball out of his mouth, as the gas in the air ignited with the fire and launched Maleficent back multiple feet.

The Main Street buildings began to burn. She got back on her feet, and she began scratching at Exton. He did the same, biting her metal exoskeleton just below her neck, and ripping out a few of her wires. She let out a scream as she bit Exton on the back, causing him to bleed. Exton let out a deep roar. As he turned around, his long muscular tale crashed into the buildings, shattering the glass, and knocking scores of bricks loose. Malefison ran into Maleficent, biting her neck below her jaw and slamming her into the burning buildings. She fell onto the pavement screaming, the buildings crumbling down upon her, making it impossible for her to get back up.

As Exton transformed back into his original form, Alana ran down Main Street to help him.

"You are better than I expected, Malefison," Maleficent beamed.

"My name is Exton, Maleficent," Exton said sarcastically.

"Here!" Alana said, as she handed him a purple sphere-shaped crystal and his magic wand.

"What's this?" Exton asked.

"I fused both of our magic crystals together, so that we could use the wand to its full potential."

They both grabbed each other's hand with the wand in the middle. They pointed it at Maleficent as they began to chant a spell in unison:

"WE BANISH YOU TO THE DARKEST REALM, TO BRING BACK TO WHAT HAS FELL, WE BOTH KNOW THAT YOU WILL DWELL, WE

RING THE BELL TO SEND YOU BACK TO YOUR CELL!"

Maleficent let out one last blood-curdling scream, as the dark purple energy flew high into the sky, bursting into brilliant fireworks the size of the entire park. As the sparks fell lower and lower, the park began to rebuild itself.

As for the Maleficent dragon, it was rebuilt and replaced on Tom Sawyer's Island for the next showing of Fantasmic.

"Wow!" Exton exclaimed.

"That was absolutely amazing," Alana agreed.

"Yeah, it really was."

Exton grabbed Alana's hand as they walked towards the train station. As they embarked the train to exit the park, the lights on the castle dimmed, as did the rest of the park. That was Disneyland's way of giving Exton and Alana a kiss goodnight.

A few minutes later, Exton teleported Alana and himself to his destroyed school.

"We have to fix this," Exton said.

"Okay, but we're gonna have to do it together."

Exton and Alana held hands as a light blue energy formed between them.

"Ready?"

"Yeah, you?"

"Yeah, let's do this," Exton said.

They blasted blue energy into the sky, and watched it burst into the size of the school. As it fell down onto the rubble of the school, it faded to a bright yellow. When sparks fell onto thousands of pieces of debris, they began to levitate. They hovered in their rightful positions, until the rest of the pieces of the school returned to their places, and then they were all re-connected.

The only thing left were the pillars in front of the school. They began to levitate much like the others. When they were finally finished, they appeared to have a thorn pattern up the entire pillar.

"Exton!" Alana said sarcastically, when she saw the concrete thorns attached to the pillars.

"What? I wanted to add a little something," Exton said, as they both laughed.

"Wait! Everyone's going to remember that I destroyed the school! What are we going to do? I can't go back to school!" Exton began to panic.

"Exton, calm down. We can just erase their memories."

"Oh, yeah," Exton chuckled.

"Ready?"

"Wait. You never told me how you got your powers," Exton said, looking befuddled.

"Let's save that for another story, shall we?" Alana said.

Exton smiled.

"Now, we have some memories to erase." They both laughed.

Exton and Alana made everyone forget what happened that day. They, however, would never forget this experience. They both agreed that whatever challenges faced them, they would be there for each other, FOREVER.